Photo: www.gezett.de/Autorenportraits.htm

Suniti Namjoshi was born in India in 1941. She worked as an officer in the Indian Administrative Service; and later moved to Canada and was Associate Professor in the Department of English at the University of Toronto for many years. She now lives and writes in Devon.

She has published numerous poems, fables, articles and reviews in anthologies, collections and journals in India, Canada, the US, Australia and Britain.

Also by Suniti Namjoshi

The Authentic Lie, 1982
From the Bedside Book of Nightmares, 1984
Feminist Fables, 1981/1993
The Conversations of Cow, 1985
Aditi and the One-eyed Monkey, 1986
The Blue Donkey Fables, 1988
Because of India: Selected Poems, 1989
The Mothers of Maya Diip, 1989
Saint Suniti and the Dragon, 1993
Building Babel, 1996 *

With Gillian Hanscombe

Flesh and Paper, 1986
Kaliyug, or Circles of Paradise, 1993

* *Building Babel* is about the process of building culture. Spinifex has put the last chapter on the Internet as the basis of a building site to which others can contribute. The URL is
http://www.spinifexpress.com.au/babelbuildingsite.htm

GOJA

AN AUTOBIOGRAPHICAL MYTH

Suniti Namjoshi

Spinifex Press Pty Ltd
504 Queensberry Street
North Melbourne, Victoria 3051
Australia
women@spinifexpress.com.au
http://www.spinifexpress.com.au

First published by Spinifex Press

Edited by Janet Mackenzie
Cover design by Tracey Anne O'Mara
Text designed and typeset in Palatino by Claire Warren
Made and printed in Australia by Australian Print Group

National Library of Australia
Cataloguing-in-Publication data:

Namjoshi, Suniti.
Goja: an autobiographical myth.

ISBN 1 875559 97 3

I. Title.

823.4

Acknowledgements

I'm grateful to the Canada Council for an Arts Grant for the completion of this book, and for their support over the years. I would also like to acknowledge my debt to Susan Hawthorne and Renate Klein of Spinifex for believing in my work. Many friends have consistently wished my writing well: my thanks are due to Juliet Davey, Christine Donald, Avril Henry, Lakshmi Holmström, Mary Meigs, Prunella Sedgwick, and Lucy White. I would also like to acknowledge my gratitude to my friend, the late Rose Elisabeth Nagelschmidt, who tried again and again to sketch a likeness of Goja for me as I described her from memory. Above all I'm grateful to Gillian Hanscombe for her literary skills and her intellectual and moral support. I found this book particularly difficult to write, and if Gill had not been there, I am not sure I would have been able to finish it.

Contents

Preface

This account is autobiographical in that my experience is all I have. It's fictional since any version manipulates facts. And it's mythical, because it's by making patterns that I make sense of all I have.

But the "facts" in this narrative are not reliable; I have chosen some, left out others. When I ask: "What really mattered?" the answer is Love or Charity. By this I mean human love: both the love that was given to me and the love I was capable of feeling. But human love, by definition, is never unadulterated. There's fear and pain, and sometimes there's bitter rage; in spite of all this, something persists. It's in this sense that my account is a quest for Charity.

For me Charity is sometimes an abstraction, sometimes a personification, often a goddess; and at times she is simply a mask or an expression that a human face might wear. Given the history of the English language, Christian overtones are inevitable in what I write. But someone with a Hindu background can create and conflate gods and goddesses and include them in the pantheon with an insouciance, which, to someone with a Christian background, can be disconcerting. However, when I do this, it is not done with disrespect.

It's difficult to capture the intensity of the experience that comes with the vision of Charity. When I was a child, I did not realise that I had been given some real love. The realisation and the understanding came much later. The two most important people in the world to me then were Goja and my grandmother. I loved them both, but the difference in their condition was so vast that it was troubling. Exploring the polarities in my life is part of my task. But above all I've written this account for my beloved dead—even when I dispute with them, even when I ask them to explain themselves, or try to explain myself to them. If my quest makes you remember and praise what was valuable in your own life, then my task will have been done.

18 November 1999
Rousdon

PART I

ONCE IN INDIA

1
GOJA

No one says that there are dreams and visions when Goja is born. There are stars in the sky, millions upon millions. There always were. And there's a *babul* tree outside the hut: visual and visible, asking as it were to be seized upon. Should I make the *babul* an emblem of Charity? The tough and twisted black tree trunk? The silver thorns? And should I make Goja an embodiment of Charity because she gave me love when I needed it most?

Goja is born in say 1900 in a small village on the Deccan plateau in western India. The sun blazes on lion-coloured land. The grass is burnt, and there isn't enough water. She nearly dies of it, of the lack of water and the dirty water. Anyway, she's female. In India it's possible to die of that. But she doesn't. Has anyone seen a *babul* sprouting? Has anyone bothered? They just grow anywhere. They must be tough.

Burping, shitting, drinking—all day long. Even Goja, who is later to become the epitome of kindness, has a mother. Babies have mothers. That's how it is, should be, well, they have someone, or should have someone. I'll endow Goja with a kindly mother, poor like her, overworked, with other children to care for, and the milk running thin in her breasts. They make do, they make out. The poor always have, or they haven't. Goja survives. Heave a sigh? The heroine has been saved? Not from Herod, just from the system. It's the same thing really.

There is a Herod: the king of the kingdom to which that particular village happens to belong. He has no sons. He's looking for sons, not killing them. The practice among Hindus is to adopt a nephew when there are no sons. Goja, of course, is not a candidate. But she is a contemporary of the real candidate, the heir to the throne, the nephew of the king. This baby—born in a house in the town nearby—this baby and Goja could be brother and sister, couldn't they? No, they couldn't. There is a divide between those who rule and those who are ruled by them, between the rich and the poor. Later, the baby informs me—the one who becomes the Ruler—that he had no mother. His mother gave him up for adoption to the Ruler of the state. No mother? Poor sod. And Goja? She had a part-time mother for five or six years; then she—Goja, not the mother—was given into service into the household of the Ruler. Was she rescued by the Ruler? By the Ruler's wife? No, no wife yet. Well, by the Ruler's steward? I don't know. I don't think Rulers or even Rulers' stewards bother very much with servant girls who are only five years old. Perhaps at the time people said that little Goja was very fortunate to be allowed to be a servant in the household of the ruler.

When you're a servant and only five years old, you sleep on the floor in the dark, and if the ladies of the house are kind to you, they let you sleep near their beds. It's to keep them company, to tell them a story, to fetch a glass of water should thirst arise. For you it's protection. For you it's a life, a place in the world. For you it's status—you've been given a function.

I heard of a lady once who was so rich or so spoilt that she had two servant women sleeping by the side of her bed: one to tell stories and the other to listen to the stories being told. Perhaps this is amusing if one is neither a lady, nor a servant?

How are these tales to be told?

They are not fairy tales. The poor sod grows up. He becomes the Rajasaheb. He was not a cipher. He was my grandfather. He was not a bad man. He—but to return to the narrative. He marries. The young woman he marries—she was named after a goddess, but aren't we all?—she becomes the Ranisaheb. She was my grandmother and I loved her. I loved her with all my heart. But I also loved Goja. And that is a problem. If I loved them both, then why was one allowed to be a queen, and why did the other one have to be a servant? If they were the two people in the whole world who gave me love when I was little, then why weren't they both allowed to be my mother? I called my grandmother "mother", but I called Goja "Goja". It was proper. I understand now that it was also deeply improper.

One day, the king, my grandfather, called me to him and told me that I must not address my grandmother in the singular. Henceforth she was to be addressed in the plural. I said the equivalent of "yes, okay"—in many ways I was an obliging child. But he didn't tell me to address Goja in the plural. If it had occurred to me to ask about that, they would have smiled. It would have been further evidence that I was a sweet child and a credit to them.

In the story the Rajasaheb and Ranisaheb have five children, four of them sons. Their eldest child is a daughter, who in turn has me for a daughter. They are all nice people. They have servants. Being kings and queens and princesses is glamorous as in fairy tales. It is also revolting. Consider the facts, which are like stony outcrops jutting out of silken water. How is it possible to be a nice person, when most of the people about you are poor? What does it mean to be a noble person when you've built your life on the lives of others? Perhaps for practical purposes all the nobility are humpbacked rich men who cannot enter the eye of heaven?

The fact is they can often be kind. They're even generous; they have the cash, the wherewithal. They also have their noble image; they like being generous. And perhaps money doesn't mean very much.

One day my grandmother gives me a bowlful of money in small change. I don't know why she has given it to me—to play with perhaps. I don't know what to do with it. As I walk down the stairs with the bowl in my hands, I spill the money. The servants pick it up. There's a strange look in their eyes. I think they think money ought not to be the plaything of children.

This Indian nobility, these Princely Rulers, were in turn ruled by the British Empress, and later by her son. In this tableau the Empress's representatives are like the grey-eyed, pink-faced monkeys the monkey man carts about, and who do a show. At least the divisions appear to be clear. Seen in this way here we all are, all on the same side: the Rajasaheb, Ranisaheb, Goja et al. against the Empress of India and her progeny, brown against white, black against pink. Well, perhaps not Goja. Why should the poor care who or what rules the whole of India or even a part of it? And perhaps not the Rajasaheb, perhaps not the Ranisaheb. After all, they've made a deal with the

Empress's lot. And besides, people should *not* be encouraged to get rid of their Rulers.

Once, when we happen to be in Delhi, and we're sitting on the grass near a statue of George V, I say to Goja that the King looks like a monkey. I suppose I must have heard one of the grownups say so. (Not my grandparents. They have to be careful.) Goja doesn't say anything. Perhaps she doesn't care whether or not the British look like monkeys, and whether or not they are driven out. Perhaps I don't care either except in theory. I'm five years old and happy chewing on a piece of grass and sitting with Goja in the morning sun.

Years later when Goja is very, very old, she sits in the kitchen peeling garlic. She wants to be useful. "Hey Goja," the family say. "You could do nothing and it would be all right." (She has worked for the family since the age of five. No one knows what age she is.) She peers upward with her one good eye. How good is it now? How much does she see? She's bent and crooked. Wasn't she always bent and crooked? What happened to her other eye? I don't know. She never told me. Why didn't she tell me? I want to hug her. Who me? (What good would that do? Might do me good.) A plump aunt says that everyone ought to be like Goja: always active, then one keeps fit.

I don't know much about Goja. And now it's too late. Goja is gone. The Ranisaheb is gone. That whole world is gone. And despite its horrors it mattered, it still matters. I'm discovering that the lives of servants go unrecorded, that the servants go unnoticed. They disappear silently—as do we all, but it should be for different reasons. It should be because of Death, because of Time. It should not be because their lives meant nothing. I've looked for a photograph of Goja, but there are none. Of the Ranisaheb there are dozens and dozens.

At night the servants dreamed their dreams. I think they must have slept a different kind of sleep. Why not? Anything is possible. They lived a different kind of life. They even smelled different. The servants smelled of food, of the hot spices in the food. I'm not sure. I think that they didn't have soap with which to wash their hands.

> The queen smells of jasmine, Goja, her servant,
> smells of common mud. But Mud is a perfume
> over which the poets have ecstasised.
> It's sold in the markets, labelled
> "the smell of rain on dry earth."
>   The queen has a bottle.
> And Goja?
>   Has nothing. The clothes she's wearing.
> No vow of poverty more penurious.

The queen and the princess are not ill-natured. When they refuse to eat meat, they do it casually. And when they send for the food that the servants have made (that is for themselves) their commands are unaffected: it happens to be a taste they happen unaffectedly to have. As for the grandchild, she likes dried fish, which makes the friends of the Ruler laugh. It is, after all, so incongruous.

At night Goja feeds dried fish to the child—dried Bombay duck. It's done out of affection. O Pelican Mother! The child knows that Goja is a servant and not her mother, but thinks that she might be a Power, and a source of love.

One day a little boy screams. He's been visiting us. He belongs to the warrior caste (like most of these nobles) and ought not to scream, but he's very little. He says the one-eyed hag has appeared before him. He means Goja. I want to hit him for finding her ugly, bent and old. But she is ugly, bent and old? No. She's bent and old because the family has used her. Because she hasn't been looked after. I should have looked after her, her slender bones.

Servants, by definition, are not supposed to be beautiful. It's not their prerogative. Many years later, when I'm grown up, a young woman servant watches me with the utmost care as I put on a sari. She is thinking that the rich know how to be beautiful.

"Your beauty derides me," says the abashed
young woman. She's a servant in the house, and only
young.
"Ah, but your beauty," replies the lady,
"is like a young sapling, a tree made of metal,
blazing and lustrous, igniting the dark, stainless—"
Which is all very well, but helps no one.

In the dark the child and Goja sleep side by side, the child on the bed, Goja on the floor; and out of pity or charity, Goja slips the child dried fish, under the mosquito net, *after the child has brushed her teeth*. The child lies there chewing the fish. Goja tells the same old story about the monkey and the crocodile:

"There was a monkey. And there was a crocodile. They were friends. The monkey lived in a jambu tree that grew along the bank of the river. The fruit of this tree was sweeter than sugar. One day the crocodile began thinking, 'That little monkey who has eaten all those jambus must have a liver sweeter than sugar.' She offered to ferry the monkey across the river . . ."

The child sleeps, Goja sleeps. Perhaps for Goja the child is not always an unmannerly nuisance, is part of the landscape, therefore familiar, therefore loved.

If Goja and the child could achieve kinship? If Goja could call the child daughter? If the child could call Goja mother? Or if they could be the same age? Slide their ages, use experience? If they could tell each other tales? Join and combine? Then Goja would think such thoughts, and the child would have Goja's experience. Lying in the dark they would speak with one voice. They would say, "Are these gods, men or monsters? Why these contrasts? Can the women be kind? Given the way they treat their servants? *If in heaven there are servants, then where do the servants live?* Surely servants servicing angels do not inhabit the same heaven? But then where do servants live? Do child & Goja bear some relation to the privileged angels?"

This is what the two would say, but then if one of the rich angels should swim into the room like a beautiful goldfish, all perfumed and in silks, if the Ranisaheb should swim into their darkness, they would be so glad. Well, the child would be glad. She would rush into the arms of the rich angel. It would be heaven, it would be the comfort of silk and crushed flowers—mogra or jasmine. There would be kisses and embraces and there would be love, oh yes, there would be love.

And what about Goja then? The smell of dried fish is not the smell of crushed white flowers, of jai or jui or queen of the night or even of jasmine. And Goja does not wear silk, she wears coarse cotton; and her body does not crush, cuddle or embrace the child. There is a distance.

There may be a distance, yells the child, but this is
a harsh landscape, where the only tree that dares
to grow regardless of water, I mean the lack of it,
is the fierce *babul*. Oh here in this arid and sunburnt
landscape, my bones are your bones, and
in the chemical analysis of your ashes and my dust
there is no difference!

* * *

Angelic Grandma swimming about is absurd, of course. She is Laxmi, goddess of peace and prosperity. She is the Ranisaheb, glittering and glorious in green and gold. She is roses, mogra, cuddles and comfort. The child loves her, but she has once seen the Ranisaheb makes Goja cry. That isn't easy. That is very difficult.

Children have an instinct for power (also for love). Their noses twitch; it works like a pheromone. They move towards power like heliotropic plants. But then what can Goja offer?

RRRectitude.

What?

Rectitude.

Meaning she is loyal to the feudals?

I know mothers weep for their sons. There are loads of pictures showing just that, painted by sons. Weeping for a daughter is more complicated. Mothers might feel they were weeping for themselves.

"Will you weep for me?" I ask Goja. (Complicated.) She is not my mother, nor even my grandmother; and ought not I to be weeping for her? But this Goja laughs, who has me for an incubus, this Goja monster, this two-headed woman who can travel through time. (Oh, we're powerful. Thus conjoined we can do anything.) The Goja Monster laughs.

"Hey," she says, "Hey, do you seriously want to be wept over, wept at, wept upon?" She gives me a comradely wink with her one good eye; and in that instant with both eyes gone, she looks like a jovial fount of wisdom. Anyway, She-I say, you were given bits of kindness. Yes, I remember I ate them up, morsels of fish, there in the dark.

And later, my grandparents' friends:
 the King's Granddaughter likes dried fish—
 food of the poor and no fit dish.
Fit for whom?
 The king's granddaughter millionth in succession,
 in consideration, divests herself of all claims.
 I will be no one. I will be nothing. And Goja and I
 will roam the landscape like the wild wind.

They shouldn't let a haloed sky god come riding—okay, flying—into the kingdom. Came anyway—my father married my mother. Very romantic. The princess has married a test pilot. But I don't think fathers should be gods. They should be ordinary bourgeois people who look after their children. Still, the princess and the pilot were very young. They wanted to travel, they wanted to be together. And I—and later the other children—could be looked after by my grandmother, and by servants and by boarding schools. I remember waiting for my parents to put in an appearance, to return from a different city, to return from America, to return from Europe, to visit me in school. After my father was killed when his plane crashed, I suppose the waiting continued. There was a recurrent dream in which he did return. It was painful. Still, some of the time we were all together.

From their point of view looking after me was Goja's function. That is what Goja was there for—Goja and boarding schools. But Goja had looked after my mother when she was little. Does that mean that I was put into the care of two grandmothers?

It would be better if the young of the species did not require quite so much attention. What do the young of the other species do? I mean of the servants? Who looks after them?

It's difficult to look at the deeds of servants. What servants have thought and felt, convention requires they keep to themselves. And history pays no attention.

It so happens that Goja saves the princess's son—he's a baby then—from an onrushing bullock cart. (No, this is not a joke. Goja really does save him. In the real world there are rich people, bullock carts, babies, servants. It's in the mind's eye that any of this is in the least exotic—or glamorous.) In consequence she breaks her arm. Forget the brackets. Goja breaks her arm. History or legend? What does Goja think? Can bullock carts rush? Is she heroic? And where are her medals?

> One day she asks for my sandals. I give
> them to her. She gives them to a grandchild.
> Someone sneers. Another day she asks
> for my sandals. I give them to her.
> She gives them to a grandchild.
> Ah Goja, had we colluded properly,
> we might have shared our extravagance.

* * *

"Hey Goja, when I was only five and a fellow servant was abusing me, where were you then?"

"I was in some other part of the landscape nursing yet another child."

Not good enough. Shouldn't mothers and grandmothers and Goja as well care what happened? The servant who abused me belonged to my parents. They had sent him along to look after me and keep me amused when I was with my grandparents. The sexual abuse was a game. There was no violence, and I didn't understand until I was nearly ten that I had been violated and that it mattered. But by then I had also understood that if I said anything I would be the one to suffer disgrace. Shortly afterwards, i.e. after the abuse, the servant was dismissed. I think he had tried to be "funny" with my mother. What I feel about him is straightforward anger. What I feel about the lack of protection is more difficult.

In the fairy tale Falada the mare says to the goosegirl: "If your mother knew/it would break her heart in two." But I suspect my mother, and all the mothers, did know or at least guessed, and that it did not break their hearts; they colluded in the disgrace. And this I cannot forgive. This hurts more than anything else.

"Hey, Goja, don't you care that this is what I think?"

"Yes, I care, but I told you. I was in another part of the landscape nursing yet another child."

Later, after I grow up, I go off to the States. "Hey, Goja, don't you mind?"

"Why should I mind? I am only a servant. And anyhow, I am not this proud, loud, wise human being you would have me be. At times I'm not even intelligent. You don't really understand what it's like."

* * *

Goja, if I become you,
    do I have to love your daughters
        and your grandson?
    Do I have to live in a small hut
        with a cowdung floor?
    Do I have to be too hot or too cold?
    Do I have to be subject to the village men?
    Do I have to be ordered around by gods, men,
        monsters and women?
    Do I have to eat less than delicious food?

Do I have to be illiterate?
Do I have to understand that there is no escape?
And that I have somehow to make my inglorious
destiny acceptable?
Goja, do I have to be humble?
And what does it mean?

I am very humble now. In the West, I am poor. Is that enough?
Or because it's involuntary, doesn't it count?

(In the delicate distance the anxious twiddle their thumbs,
and here I am willing to make a beauty out of sorrow.)

First the mud and murk, then the king and queen, their faces emerging, and Goja, of course; then one daughter, four sons, and Goja, of course; then the grandchildren, and Goja. Always Goja?

How would the rich manage without their servants?
It's not just that they can't tie their shoelaces—
they could wear sandals.
They can't cook their own dinners.
They can't baby-sit their own children.
They can't—oh they can't anything:
till their own fields,
do their own mending,
buy their own groceries,
wash their own dishes,
make their own beds.
They can lie on their own beds and that's about it,
and some of them, can sometimes be giddy and gracious.

Is their downfall—a whole set of warriors rolling downhill to death and dissolution—a true epic? Or a true tragedy: kings and queens deprived of status? Perhaps the true tragedy is the life and death of a solitary servant? Better seen possibly as a true comedy? Goja reigning in Dante's heaven. Why not? It's not a joke.

In 1948, the year after Independence, Sardar Vallabhai Patel amalgamated the Princely States. Their income was reduced considerably, and later, much later, under Pandit Nehru, or possibly his daughter, their privy purses were cut off entirely. Like cutting off tails! Ridiculous.

Is it the same kind of rubbishing when Goja is made to tumble down, I mean bow down—was it involuntary?—and I am made to be of little account. Does *that* lead to humility? Did the Princes feel it? Was Goja humble? Am I proud? When I was a child, they were very keen on rank, these Indian nobles. They still are, even now fifty years later, when their ranks mean very little. Part of the training in manners was learning exactly who merited which type of salutation, whose feet it was necessary to touch, who deserved to be bowed down to and then greeted, and who merited an ordinary greeting (a *namaskar*), and who deserved none at all except in response.

Pride is a great sustainer of persons.

When I grew up and chose to go abroad, I remember the contempt spilling from my mother's tongue. "Go abroad? There you'll be nothing and no one. A third-class citizen!"

Goja? Since you did not deserve any salutation at all, were you nothing and no one? And here in the West, so many years later, since I am "triply oppressed", as a kindly, Western, liberal woman once informed me—as a woman, a lesbian and a brown-skinned person—am I less than nothing? It makes me want to laugh. To be nothing is to be free.

The blood-stained hands of the Emperor
Sikander, of the Emperor Asoka, of any
old emperor, do not horrify,
since poets have been ad men to princes,
and historians chroniclers of the crooked and bold.
So then what's the difference between the queen
and her servant? Oh it's a quantitative difference,
and quantities of money make a different world.

Is it fair to compare suffering, Goja? What were your griefs? Unannotated? Not noted. Married young? Happily or not? No husband? A husband dead? Did it matter? There was some mention of unimportant daughters and a much-loved grandson. (In which case, Goja, what would it have profited me to have been your daughter?) But Goja? Are you in fact my grandmother's sister? Unequal in rank, but equal at bottom, because men rule —okay? NOT OKAY! Would either of you have agreed with me? My unwillingness to serve? Is the willingness to rule any better? There are so many voices.

Oh I have a million things to do, but my cousins are calling: Dhrtirashtra's offspring, seeking to be kings.

Well, I don't see why I can't be king or queen or something of the sort. It's very nice to be bowed down to. A little respect is all I want: "street-cred", as the thug said in the street.

* * *

Meanwhile, we can be proud, pompous, anything. In relation to "them" we are all "we", because we've gone on and on for forty centuries. The Westerners keep quiet because of racism. Or they're afraid someone might say, it all has to do with the history of colonies. Yet, there's this: it takes a Mother Teresa to observe there are people lying on the street. And she does something, however charmless and unsatisfactory, at least she does it.

The truth is—everyone knows it, no one contradicts it—that it's not civilised to have this crass disparity between the poor and the rich. Nothing changes. We all carry on. Poets tell lies.

> I wanted so much to make something beautiful
> for a most loving and much loved woman.
>
> Those who once lived are burnt or buried,
> but these two dead trot in my head
> in a wakeful afterlife, so that I have
> not one, but two, not two, but three
> —three monstrous heads?
>   Let the sleeping dead
> sleep. Well, they do sleep, but are not averse
> to occasional chat in the deep and backward abyss.

Goja says: "We all went over the hill, you know. We all went over the hill. The King, the Queen and I, their servant. And since we all went so merrily over the hill, with such jollity, such inevitability, we might as well have gone all holding hands." Then she turns on me, "I don't know what you're trying to deconstruct. Or why. Can't you see? Don't you see? Death does such a thorough job. It deconstructs the flesh, all the atoms. It deconstructs time. It deconstructs us. Why don't you carry us about, all wrapped up, cuddly and coddled, like so many papooses?"

What did Goja and the Ranisaheb say to each other? No, not in real life. After their deaths, in limbo? The Ranisaheb was unregenerate, unthinking, anyway. She said to Goja, "Wash my feet, run my bath, iron my clothes, sweep my room." What did Goja do? Did she refuse? I mean was she allowed to refuse if she was Charity incarnate? Yes, Goja refused. She explained charitably that being so frightfully selfish and dependent was bad for the Ranisaheb. Of course, the Ranisaheb didn't understand. But perhaps in limbo she did understand.

Perhaps they sat about discussing the manner of their deaths, i.e. of their actual cremation, their respective pyres?

"Mine was made up of sandalwood," said the Ranisaheb.

"Mine of bits of *babul* wood," replied Goja. "There was barely enough. Luckily I'm thin."

Perhaps they both chortled? Thin Goja and fat Ranisaheb?

When the Ranisaheb and Goja converse together, which of them is Lady Charity? Which Lady Generosity? Is it all nonsense? Can they only speak as equals after they're dead? And by that time is it meaningless?

Suppose Goja met me on an arid plain and scolded, "What are you doing, you silly child?" Suppose I explained I was deconstructing "Victory": the power and the glory of the robber barons, her feudal overlords. Suppose then that Goja drew herself up: "But I too am upper-caste . . ." Surely she would not? Goja the Wise, Goja the Good? Mythologised and so saintly that—?

In the end I said to Goja, "Okay, what's your claim to fame?"

She started laughing. "You!" she giggled. "You've sanctified me!"

"What's the problem?" I asked. "Don't you want to be Sweet Sister Charity?"

She peered at me like a wily owl. "That's exactly who I have been."

"Well, but—I'll make Charity young and beautiful. I'll make Charity sexy."

Goja said, "You be Charity."

"Don't want to be Charity," I wailed. "I haven't suffered enough. I am not worthy."

"Oh, you've probably suffered a bit in your time," Goja replied quite kindly.

Later, in the interests of justice, I remarked, "The whole object of this exercise is for Goja to become Queen."

"Nonsense," said the Queen, quoting Confucius unconsciously, "the whole object of this exercise is for Queen to be Queen, Goja to be Goja, everyone to observe rank and precedence, and to be happy."

"Yes, well," said Goja, her one eye glinting. "I don't really want to upset anybody, but perhaps—"

On that occasion she did not finish what she might have said.

What might she have said? I could ask her. Would she say it? Could I invent it?

> "Look," she said, "I'm tired of all this heart
> raking. You get a little bit of life
> like the sparrow flitting in the Great Hall.
>   Then it's over.
> That's all it is. That's all."
>   "Therefore?" I asked.
> "Oh, seize the day. Do what you like.
> Have a great holiday. The point is
> in limbo it's cold and I'm tired of it all."

How then? What might I understand? Would it go like this?

Once upon a time there was a king who was not naked. He had fine robes. Everyone and anyone with any taste at all, with any eyes at all, admired these robes. And anyone and everyone with any brains at all, wanted to be king, and wanted those robes. So that when a stupid child—a would-be poet—said loudly that the king was naked, they very properly and justly locked this person up, since it was obvious that the king was clothed. It was also obvious that the poet / pauper / child had a malicious gleam in her eye and wanted to see the king disrobed. They asked her why.

"Because," she answered, "I want to show you that power is not glamorous."

"But it is," they said.

"Well, then I want to show you that power doesn't matter."

"But it does," they cried. "Power does matter. We can prove it to you."

With that they stripped her to demonstrate that emperors are gorgeous and the powerless go naked.

"Nevertheless," she muttered, "nevertheless, the sun stands still. The earth does move. And emperors without their robes do go naked."

"Oh, well, yes," they said. "We agree with you. That's why it's so important not to show the Emperor disrobed."

Later, with the help of Charity, she bought some clothes.

These things happen. It's best probably to cry for everyone; then ask the earth how it sustains so much grief? And how this land with the lion-coloured grass swallows the pain? Why it's silent?

2
FAIRY TALE

Things happen in the silence.

Sometimes the axe murderer comes along and wields his axe so decisively that you can see the bodies lying there, split in half. No, not dead, still living. And for the rest of their lives they bleed.

Sometimes the axe murderer wields his axe like a paring knife. Slivers of skin are so finely shaved, you can barely see the flesh, barely feel the bleeding. And this too goes on for the rest of your life.

It's not that children don't suffer, or that princesses don't suffer, or that the daughters of princesses don't suffer. They suffer all right, and the suffering becomes a source of fear, more pervasive, more mortal, than the first injury. Those who should have protected you, failed to protect you, and that makes them angry. You know they know. You know you'd get hurt if you ever said anything. Their fear infects. When this happens the tale can only be told as a fairy tale, as a long and impossibly tall story, such as, for example, the story of

THE BLACK PIGLET AND THE QUEEN OF SPADES

One day the Queen of Spades looked so long and lovingly into the mirror that she decided she was real. Such faith, such truth, such belief—in what?—in MYSELF. The answer came with the sound of thunder. "I am who I am. And that I am the Queen of Spades is widely acknowledged." She summoned her courtiers. Some came. If she was the queen, then that made them kings, earls, lesser-ranking nobles, possibly knaves, but so what, the Queen was offering . . . something? Half her kingdom? Her hand in marriage? Herself? Her body to be given to her only begotten sons? Daughters? Kill as catch can. The deck of cards flew upon her. And the Queen? Ah yes, she was still the Queen. A deck of cards can do very little. She had achieved? Credibility! And the courtiers? Well, they bled a little; but that too was proof that they were more than mirages and less than mortal.

"What is the Queen doing?"
"Chasing piglets."
"A Queen chasing piglets?"
"Like the farmer's wife. She will cut off—"
"Piglets as black as spades?"
"They are the Queen of Spades' piglets."
"Why are the piglets crying?"
"Oh, come off it. Everybody knows the piggies are dying."

At the Queen of Spades' funeral, her four children took up their poses. One squeaked, "What will become of me? Alas, what will become of me?" One roared, oh his roar was the roar of a bull, castrated in his very prime. One wept. "I am the Good Son. The Unprodigal Son. The Good Brother. The Good Father. Possibly the Good Husband. And anyway, I am all in all the Good One. And I am unloved, because my mother hasn't loved me. Well, not long enough, not well enough, and now she has up and gone and died." And the one who wanted to be big and bold decided that she herself was dying. She saw those fragile bones, that bitter exterior, and she saw her fear mirroring fear. She saw a knife with two blades and no handle. She saw the Queen of Spades doubled and redoubled. Swords both ways. "If she dies, you die," the mirrors told her. And the Queen of Spades reached out and whispered, "Live as I have lived in the Hall of Mirrors, in the Hall of Swords, in the Hall of Suffering. Reach for suicide and finally achieve it. May you die my death." Which this last and most imaginative one very nearly did; but then invented a different tale.

Little daughter meek and mild,
Someone fucked you as a child.
I am both vengeance and fate.
I am the one you hate.
I am the one who will kill you to death,
O you who mirror my fearfulness.

But in this Nightmare, Mother,
Who is the other?
Who eats and sleeps and breathes,
and watches telly for a little happiness?

This poor woman went to market and was bought and sold.

"Then," said Piglet, "I am a brave knight. I am off to fight the Queen of Spades. She will stick a sword into me. She will gouge my skin—I have no armour—with slivers of glass, with broken mirrors, she will skin me, and she will do it inexpertly."

"Oh me, oh my," cried Piglet, weeping by the wayside.

"Come now, sweetie," roared a Chance Wayfarer. "Get thee to a therapist! We have all been damaged by Mummy the

Murderess. What's the rest of your tale?"

"My tail's been cut off," Piglet nearly yelped. Thought better of it. "The rest of my tale, Sir Wayfarer," said Piglet with dignity, "is that the Queen dons my own flayed skin and is utterly transformed, is no longer Queen. And as for me, I am free."

"Hmm," muttered Wayfarer, who did not consider this a Happy Ending.

When the small rain came raining down
and did not damage my face, I thought,
"This is a clement climate. Here malice
is impersonal. I am not somebody's daughter,
and she will not seek me out in the alien
corn where I have built my nest."

One day Piglet sat gazing in the mirror and suffered a dreadful metamorphosis—smiling back at her, looking both maudlin and melancholy, was the dreaded Queen of Spades. Piglet wanted to deconstruct herself, to reconstruct herself, to dissolve if need be. But dissolution is death.

Said Piglet thoughtfully, "The Queen of Spades and the Black Piglet are they the same? The Queen of Spades and the Black Piglet are different. One sticks the pig. The other is the pig. The pig squeals. The Queen of Spades and the Black Piglet inhabit the same body. Two bodies? No, my body. This monster I have made from my own imaginings. Alas, alack, woe, sorrow, woe and company. If the Piglet put on the Queen's accoutrements? If the Queen was killed by her own sword? What? Kill my mother? But the Queen of Spades is not my mother. She is a painted dragon, devil. She is a playing card, which must not be played. No fantasy this, but a nightmare made up of blood and guts and childhood fear. The

Queen of Spades will find me out and offer me up to the gods that be, to the fighting, fucking, powerful men—of whom she is afraid. Ma won't and didn't protect me! Let that go screeching down the corridors of fame."

"Once upon a time," said Piglet, making up yet another tale, "there was a great artist, who could conjure up such powerful images of horror and terror that she died of fright."

The Piglet dancing in the moonlight imagined herself dancing, imagined the Queen. She crowed, "If I can imagine all this, I can imagine anything!" She imagined Victory! And was discontent. Then she knew she had to imagine what to imagine.

The Black Queen had her own imaginings. She thought of murder and martyrdom, of four little piglets tugging at her teats. Such images would make a sow out of her. She thought instead of romance and happiness, of what might have been, and WASN'T! The four little piglets had turned her into a Farmer's Wife. She acquired more piglets: with enough animals, she could rule again. The farm animals begged for food. Shoving scraps into the troughs of hungry pigs was an unfitting occupation. Nevertheless, she would humble herself. Pigs too must be permitted to live. And was she not the Queen of Pigs? The Pig Princess? But the piglets were ungrateful; she experienced weariness. Let them eat cake, let them eat apples, or roast pork and dumplings. She would distance herself.

But these were the imaginings of the Black Pig, the turn-tail pig, cowering in the shadows, and also trying to distance herself.

"Come along," says the Piglet. "You are not the Queen of Spades and I am not a Pig. We are two women who have been permitted to live. Death is long. Life is sweet. Why not make the best of it?"

"You make the best of it," says the haughty Queen.

"Come off it," says the Piglet. "Don't primp, don't pose, don't attitudinise. You are only a human being."

"Yes," says Queenie. "That's what I am. And you refuse to recognise it."

"It's my specs," says the Pig. "It's the looking-glass. It's something to do with optics. But yes, you're human. You have your foibles and frailties."

"And my humanity!" says Queenie sharply.

In the difficult and unreachable wastes of the tundra, the Queen of Spades perches on an ice floe. "Ice is nice," she murmurs. No, that's not what she says. "Ice is barren and beautiful. Ice shall preserve the prince in the glass. Ice the frozen and inimitable past. Ice carved with patience and craft, ice shall outlast. And I, frozen in grief, haloed by snow, glazed by sorrow, I shall be my own monument."

Four little piglets make tracks in the snow, smudged and illegible and semi-illiterate. The snow and wind will cover them up. The snow and wind will, some day, wrap everything up. But right now, the four little piggies lack something. A greater translucence, a certain dignity? Even so, four glass piglets make a fine and plausible show.

The Black Piglet fashions a mask, half a dozen masks, and suitable skins to go with them. She will be a monkey, donkey, or possibly a lioness. No, no more diversions. She will be who she always was. She's approaching the truth. She's approaching a wall. *O mirror, mirror?* But the mirror can offer no absolute truths, only the picture of a Black Sow.

"I am too good for this world," moaned the Black Piglet. "Me too. I am too good also," moaned the Black Queen. "Right," said the Hog Keepers and helped them along.

Experiment

Set up a dark room and a mirror. Let a beam of light hit the mirror. Oh, and right at the back there's another mirror. As Piglet approaches the first mirror, she sees her back in the second mirror, receding gradually. As Piglet backs from the first mirror she sees herself travelling through time. The distance travelled must be considerable. Time has passed. Her watch says so. She should have arrived. But the dark room is still dark. It would have been helpful to have known at the outset where she was going. It would have been helpful to have understood mathematics: Isaac Newton, Lewis Carroll, even Albert Einstein. She has done something wrong. She could sit still. She could open the dark room and spoil the images. She could take up painting. She could fix all the pictures in their proper solution and leave. It's puzzling. The beam of light, doubled and redoubled, should have achieved enlightenment. It should have been dazzling!

Piglet tries a different experiment. She substitutes a playing card, a very large one, for one of the mirrors, and creeps up slowly with a knife in her hand. Now there's trickery. Behind her Piglet approaches Piglet with a knife. Before her Queenie approaches Queenie with a knife. Piglet laughs. Queenie laughs. They exchange masks. They even exchange their favourite skins. Two little girls say "Boo!" to each other. They run up and down. They break a mirror. Piglet trips on a piece of glass. "It's only a cut. I guess I'll live." She swaggers about. Bravery or Bravado? Well, why not?

But after all these clever experiments Piglet's still bleeding. Who will pick her up? Tell her it's okay? She has no godmothers. Doesn't much like them. They're frilly and silly; they simper in the dark. But she needs someone. Anybody there? Anyone lurking? Me, I'm out there. Who? Me. Behind Piglet's mask reality crashes. It's all right, little one. You and I together, we'll absorb the pastness of the past.

It's not just a question of two little girls playing happily together. I now have to rip off my own mask. What's exposed? "A blank, my lord." Or something else? Flesh and a skull. A skinned face.

Decorum requires? Help me, Piglet! I helped you when you were frightened. I'll acquire skin. I'll acquire features. Soon, I'll acquire a pleasant smile. Meanwhile, Piglet, put together a makeshift mask—reasonably genuine and tough enough.

Piglet at work
I will free-float gladly as flowers do, Mother.
Flowers are rooted.
I will penetrate the lattice of air, Mother.
Air is amorphous. You will be nothing.
I will create a beautiful body, Mother.
You have one already—of my giving.
Well, then I will inhabit my own body,
I will occupy space,
I will own my face,
And when I'm tired, I'll fall asleep.
Exeunt omnes.

3
THE NEEDY

Oh the drip-drop rain will slit my heart,
let dormant seedlings rage and whine. Then
who will rise from the mud, the oozy
lake, the slime?
Dead fathers,
neither forgotten, nor forgiven.
Live grandmothers,
frightening and frivolous, in their prime.
Unmourned corpses,
not still as photographs, but live as telly,
prancing and poncing on borrowed time.
A crowd, a host, of noisy revellers,
not letting me in, not letting me go,
driving and shoving through native soil.

A resolution to inhabit my own body is all very well, but hardly necessary. The body is inhabited anyway. The body is infested. The Goja-monster, the Raja-monster, the Goldfish-monster, the Mummy-monster, the Daddy-monster, everyone I've ever known takes root, grubs for sustenance, even the servant who molested me. Can I live with that? Even the labourer I injured later, years later, in an accident? Even the children who injured me. All these people are jostling one another, entering into me, living with me. I am an ark. All these people I repudiate are part of me. *They are me.* It's not just a case of Mummy Bear, Daddy Bear and little Goldilocks, alias Baby Bear, though these three are, of course, prolific in their mutations and permutations. They agitate, cogitate, are needy in their mewlings, and their silence. They never did grow up, or if they did, they all grew at a different rate; and they all stubbornly refused to change. They were silly. They *are* silly. Time changed them anyhow—dragged them howling through degrees of change. But when they aren't crying, they see their refusal as an act of defiance. This helps them to forget they need to change, but then that would be frightening.

And so they come: The Child, The Knight and The Woman, and they tell lies. Each disguises the child within, but it's there and someone has to wipe the snot from its nose, the tears from its eyes. They cannot be persuaded to take turns. They cannot be persuaded that there is any need, but the need is there, and the unfulfilled need causes suffering. Therefore, out of need, they speak to one another and sometimes to the child.

What the Child Said

Everyone carries a child, who, if allowed
to emerge unhurt, goes skipping merrily
across the countryside, for the time being
safe, albeit self-conscious. Then why not love
this wretched child? It wants to be loved,
and its need is not unreasonable.

What the Woman and the Child Said

Perhaps you need more than I am able to give?

Of course I need more. More, more, more, yelps the child. But certain truths ought not to be told, are not politic, nor poetic, are not good manners. Only an imbecile would admit to need, or a fool, or a beggar, or a child. But then I do not have the privileges of a child.

What privileges?

Oh well, you know—pleading helplessness, denying aggression, alleging innocence . . .

Why not?

Because then I would have to be innocent.

And powerless?

Yeah. All that. Anyway, I don't need anything. I'm not asking for anything. I don't want anything.

Of course, you want something. That's why you're here, at this moment, in this place of need.

Okay, I want to be loved.

Loved?

Yes, you know, kissed, coddled, cuddled, admired, made much of, succoured and suckled, put to bed and cradled in sleep.

I see. You want to be mothered?

Yes, mothered, but not bossed. Mothered, but not bossed. I want to be the one in charge you see.

Sex?

Yeah. Sex with a tinge of incest thrown in.

But not real incest?

Er, well, let us consider incest. Let us be intellectual. The meaning of the thing. Why the taboo? It must, of course, be to prevent humans from behaving like babies. Dangerous things, grown-up babies.

Men, you mean?

Well, yes. But a line has to be drawn. Somewhere a line.

I see. And what's our line?

You have to draw it.

Well, no sex at all. We are related if you please.

Incestuously?

Don't be silly, but I take your point We can still discuss, dissect and theorise.

Right!

Where were we then? If you had sex, what would it mean?

Romance and the gibbering of monkeys. The golden apples well within reach.

My dear! I do not know how to make something beautiful out of need.

Tell lies.

Both truth and lies?

Yes, a judicious admixture.

I shall do as the poets do.

Yes. Stare at your need.

And out of the darkness engender something?

Yes, why not? The lady is a poet. Poetry, passionate poetry, emerging out of need is not the prerogative of men and babies.

And so sometimes there are transformations and the mother becomes a poet and the child becomes a mother.

WHAT THE CHILD NOTED

Out of need
        windmills are turned into giants.
        Money is invented.
        Women are raped.
                Children are raped.

Sometimes, men are raped.
Prodigies are raised.
Taj Mahals, colossi, and pyramids built.
Friends are swindled.
Enemies killed.
Humility is achieved.
Also humiliation.
And out of need
entire forests are turned into paper.
And on some of this paper.
poems are inscribed.

"Out of need," you say?
Yes, said the child, looking uncommonly old and wise.

What the Knight and the Child Said

The Knight mumbled:
I thought need was ignoble, incapable, puny. But Need is a dragon and a demon, capable of almost anything. How can this be?
The Child said:
My need is a cavity which I explore with the tip of my tongue.
The Knight said:
I am not used to parenting; the Motherhood of Men makes me queasy.
The Child said:
Well, that's my problem, isn't it?

Having settled all that, the Knight and the Lady turned to each other.

Duet

We drink up need in small paper cups, while comparing flavours amicably.

"Mine's quite brackish."

"Ah no, yours is smooth. I think in time it could prove addictive?" This is said shyly, and one or the other smiles wryly.

We remember to maintain levity.

Having tasted need we can now discuss its shape and size.

"Your need is like fire . . ."

"The problem is it's hard to hold—and dangerous."

We commiserate. "My own is an absence . . ."

"No doubt lovely."

"But how embrace a hollow shape?" We shake our heads,

sigh with sad complacency.

And then there's the sound of our common need.

"Yours is dulcet."

"As is yours. Perhaps we could sing in harmony?"

"My voice is untrained—"

"Therefore sincere."

"Do you know what song the sirens sang?"

"According to the poets they sang all day and all night long,

'Help! O please, help me!'"

"May we not vouchsafe ourselves a Vision of our Need?

"You are she!"

"What I the untidy, the ungraceful?!!!"

"No. No. No. I was only joking. Don't be silly." Huge relief.

Then nicely, amid much mirth and hilarity, we explain to each other that visions

are generally lacking in clarity.

And last, the odour of our need? Sandalwood and incense?

Yes, why not, till suddenly, one of us whispers, "My need stinks! A definite stench—not unfamiliar."

"Yeah. So does mine."

Both of us grin. "Let's shake on it! Lear smelt it;
he called it mortality."

What They All Sang Once They Had Wiped their Noses

Villanelle Asking Nothing

To be properly grateful is to ask for nothing at all.
Does the light grace a beloved head?
Let the light fall where it chooses to fall.

The roses have grown ten feet tall.
I shall gather none, neither the white, nor the red,
since to be properly grateful is to want for nothing at all.

Perhaps once—before the fall—
truth and desire might have wed;
but now—the light must fall where it chances to fall.

In a dream I asked, "Did you call?"
In the dream you smiled, shook your head.
I was properly grateful for nothing at all.

To know what is best is best of all:
nothing to do, less to be said.
Let the daylight fall when it chooses to fall.

Roses have climbed a broken wall,
some lie slaughtered, some half dead.
To be properly grateful is to ask for nothing at all.
Let the light fall where it chances to fall.

They've said their piece and sung their song. Now they bow and nod to Charity, whom they have personified, and who, they hope, will mother them all. And she, not really knowing what she might say, tells them they have done very well, and they are all good children.

But I, the spokesperson for the horde, the one with the speaking tongue (while the rest gibber), turn on Charity. There are questions to be asked, answers to be solicited. Is she one of us? That's one. Will she too come aboard the ark? That's another. And do we want her? That's a third. And perhaps it can't all be done in one sitting, but we could get started. Whose face does she have? What mask does she wear? And when, in the course of our experience, has she manifested herself? She might not answer, but at least I can ask.

4
ABOUT SUFFERING

Love did not say, "Come, little one,
I will remove all pain."
Love said, "I will show you how to make
the best use of suffering—
so that it's efficacious."
I said, "Love, do you know what
you're about?
And Love said, "Not always."

Once I have summoned all my inhabitants and seen them milling about me like noisy schoolchildren, I realise that I am their teacher, that I am in some relation of authority to them. And when I see my own snotty face among that lot at the age of ten, eleven, twelve, thirteen, eating too much, reading too much, somehow able to digest it all, but unable to get socialised properly, I think, ah yes, perhaps I am supposed to be Charity herself, or a version of her, Love, dancing and smiling, even mischievous (and in the Christian version even slaughtered). Perhaps I am supposed to embrace them and effect some sort of reconciliation?

Suffer the little children . . . But the children are so ill-natured . . .

"We are not what you've internalised," they all say, still looking unconscionably like children. "We have a life of our own." I want to scatter them like ninepins. They look so pleased—despite disclaimers, despite protests—that they have had such an influence.

They are like a bunch of children, like a bunch of school-children I once knew.

And Goja flat on her back in the sun, opening her one good eye, seems unconcerned: "You want to de-glamorise power, Sweetie, you'll first have to deconstruct it within yourself." It is presumably an oracular titbit, a present.

* * *

In the early fifties I was sent to an American boarding school in the Himalayan foothills. In the "real world" the Korean War was being fought. In the school I'd been sent to the Americans were thumping their chests, or, more demurely, their breasts, and proclaiming loudly that at anything and everything Americans were best. I was very unhappy at this school, not passionately unhappy, not greatly or beautifully unhappy, it was just a dreary unhappiness, like the monsoon, when the sky is always grey—you don't need a forecast—and the rain drips down.

"They have pink faces and their hair is made of metal," I say to my mother, "Please take me home. I cannot stay here. I cannot understand a word they are saying." I am sure I say this clearly enough to be understood by her.

My mother replies, "Soon you will speak exactly like them—that is permissible, though a more English accent would be preferable. Learn what they have to teach you, but never become one of them. That is not permissible." Does she really say this? Yes. Because I know that I am supposed to learn English without becoming Anglicised (or Americanised), that I am supposed to let the words of the Bible flow over my ears without becoming Christianised. Difficult. Also very easy, since they teach such a shoddy brand of Christianity. And yet that's where I'm told about Charity, that the greatest is Charity—and that by a man it's hard to like. (Whatever he was, St Paul *wasn't* likeable.) And yet it sticks?

If you're not a Christian, the teachers make it clear, you will go to hell. But they don't try very hard to convert the few Indians, who are mostly Hindu or Muslim, because that would cause a scandal. I consider hell. Blue fires. For five long minutes I consider hell, and I'm frightened. Then I dismiss it. It's not a matter of empirical proof. I'm not old enough to understand empiricism. It's just that I can't see why God would trouble to be so awful. My parents haven't been awful, they haven't been wilfully and gratuitously punitive. I doubt very much that they would burn me in hell, or would even want to. So then why would God?

It's so easy to cover up the cracks, paper contradiction. In that school I was in hell. Someone wilfully and gratuitously put me there. But that's a whisper—and not one that at the time I could afford to hear.

As I try to write about dreary adolescence and cruel adolescents, my beloved cat falls ill and dies. Will she too become one of my ghosts? An inhabitant of the ark? How will she fare among clamorous humans? I do not want to lock her in. She, at least, should be free, able to come and go—alien, with topaz eyes.

It was during this period that my father's plane crashed. He was a test pilot. He must have risen early in the morning and gone to the aerodrome. Then he must have climbed into the cockpit of the small trainer the factory had built and risen into the air. But his plane got caught in someone else's jet stream. Down, down, down, he must have come twirling down. I had wanted so much to be with him, and I had wanted my parents to be together again (they were living apart). I had managed to run away from school legally, by writing to my mother and my grandparents week after week, but he crashed before I saw him. After that I went back to that school for another year.

Does realism matter? What it was like then? The taste of the monsoon in a Himalayan hill station? Absence matters. His absence. And now the death of my companion the cat. Can a cat matter so much? Yes. Ridiculous—that they prosecute people when they should prosecute death.

When I gather the *dramatis personae*, some are internal and some are external—they take on each other's faces—and some are both. They don't stay the same. They change their age. It's frightening to think, despite all this talk of sacrosanct identity and the integrity of the personality, that we are all composites, that we are all parts of each other. Horrible! Someone else's nose stuck on my face. A medley of different bodies, of different personalities, and these in constant flux as well. No, not multiple personalities politely taking turns. A mishmash speaking with one voice, and not even realising that the voice is garbled. And this mishmash is called sanity. Well, why not?

The theatre for the *personae* is a clearing in the Himalayan foothills. It is obviously an amphitheatre. The steep sides of the hills and valleys make that plain as do the snowclad Himalayan peaks, aloof and in the distance. The Himalayan peaks can be gods or giants or the real adults, watching what happens. The action is in my memory, but it "happened". An amphitheatre is the proper setting. All is mimetic. All is as it should be. And the escape hatch has been properly set up: I might be lying, creating a fiction. The actors are schoolchildren, former tormentors. Once they had names. Later their names, their noses, their faces, will belong to others. Faces change, but masks remain. Two of the teachers, Miss M and Mrs C, had the face of Charity. The mask of Charity?

There must have been something wrong with me. I had my nose in the air. I laughed—a most musical laugh. I read books. I had my nose in a book. I didn't seem to care what other people thought, what the group thought. *I didn't care what the group thought.* Ah yes, that was my crime. I didn't understand I was supposed to fit in. Why not? I don't know. I was ostracised. Didn't that teach me? No. I walked alone. I thought I had no choice. Perhaps I had no choice. I played alone. No choice. I talked to ants. A sharper lesson was necessary. A dozen of them jumped on me, caught me by the arms and legs and swung me about. As they did this, they kept kissing me. They were like reptiles pecking at their prey—like *maenads*. They were civilised little girls. Who had taught them the tactics of gangs? Be! Be what? Be heterosexual! Be Christian! Be American! Be! Be like them? No, not that. Wanting would have been enough. Wanting would have been better. You must want to be like us. That would be satisfactory. But to fail to want to be like them? That constitutes contempt, and the jury pounces—like a pack of cards. But it hurt. If hell had existed, they would have enjoyed being there, devising tortures and cunning snares. I would not serve, therefore the devils tormented their fellow, another poor devil, in a created hell. I remember the pain, though at the time I half denied it. But the pain was there—and the shame and disgrace of being slobbered upon.

Wasn't anything good? Yes. Mrs C teaching me how to get at square roots even though it wasn't necessary. And Miss M telling me, startlingly, without warning, as we were standing in the queue before dinner time, that I was a brick. The others laughed

Which of their faces was my face? Where did I wander? Goosey? Goosey? Did I bash anyone? *Ah yes, I must have done. / But that psychodrama belongs to someone / weeping beneath a different sun.* No one on purpose. There were more of them; they won. I suppose they either had to do what I said: read books, be good at sports, ignore boys. Or they had to do what they said: wear matching clothes, compete for boys, gain status. They did what they said. What hurt? The deliberate bashing or the isolation? Both. I do not wish them well. I've borrowed their faces. And with all the cruelty they bestowed on me I wish them ill. But these are not the main characters.

So then who is lurking behind the scenes, behind the arras, behind the masks?

These have no names. They are the mob: the vicious ones with sharp teeth, little knives and their eye on the main chance—in subsequent experience encountered often, but in ones and in twos easily shrugged off. I hate them.

Then there are the leeches. They are not bleeding—they may have bled once—but they profess weakness, and they latch on. I hate them too. Puling parasites! Limpets!

And finally there's Queenie and her lot: the gods on their mountain tops, or on the plains below, not even watching the drama. They dumped me in it. *(Aha! The therapist pounces.)* I hate—But it's not much use cursing the gods, the important adults, and it might be dangerous.

"I will do such things,—What they are yet I know not,—but they shall be the terrors of the earth." Lear is the tragedy of a young person. Well, of a powerless person. Once begun, a litany of hate is easy to pronounce.

If for me that was hell, and if my fellow schoolchildren were the inhabitants of hell, then I must record that hell was damp, mountainous and admittedly beautiful.

And those responsible for putting me in hell? The gods, the real protagonists? The important adults? The gods weren't there. Nor were they standing lone and significant on the mountaintops, on the snowclad peaks, watching everything from a suitable distance in suitable grandeur. The gods were on the plains—the fertile Indo-Gangetic plains, or on the Deccan plateau, or in Europe, enjoying themselves. Perhaps they were tearing themselves to pieces? What can a child know about what the gods do to themselves and to each other?

Shale, soil, and roads carved out of the steep hillside, and the moss, always the moss, the dark, soft, emerald moss, which was no comfort, and the ferns, maidenhair ferns, bearded Christmas ferns, whose names we were supposed to memorise: that was how it was. Sometimes the path was only one foot wide, and the valley was hundreds, no, thousands of feet, below. *Dangerous!* The rhododendron trees—trees, not shrubs, with brittle branches—had red flowers. There were pines, firs, cedars, oaks—dentiferous oaks (also memorised). The smell of pine meant nine months of exile. The autumn leaves falling measured the days till Going Down Day. The winter line, a bar of orange along the horizon, only meant it was getting colder, but not winter yet, which was when we could return to the family bosom. I did not learn to be loving there. Nor did I learn how to do without love. I learnt how to suffer, but not very well: a degree of self-pity, a touch of stoicism, and considerable rage, inchoate and well hidden.

When I cannot see my own face, is it likely that I might see yours, O Sister Charity? For them I had the face of a racoon. (Horn-rimmed specs.) For them I was beyond the pale. No boyfriends then, and none acquired. For them? I was an object of charity. Someone to be kind to, to be invited out, and that they were being kind was made plain. What they offered was like a lumpy porridge, cold and lumpy, and not even nutritious.

But there were, after all, two faces there. Does Charity appear in fits and starts?

A different thought. I have inherited them all, every single one, even the worst of them, the most despicable.

I had thought that Charity would be allied to dearth, that perhaps she rose out of suffering like Aphrodite out of the sea. And I worried about whether Charity could be beautiful, and about her relation to Aphrodite. (Is Princess Diana deified, a popular version of Charity made sexy?) I don't know how Charity is generated, but I do know that hatred is born out of suffering. And out of not-suffering? Indifference is born.

But sometimes the bashed-up one becomes reluctant to do unto others what has been done to her. Is that when Charity is born? And when well-being and not-suffering do not generate indifference? Is that the other miracle?

Or is Charity self-begotten? Have suffering and not-suffering little or nothing to do with her? Suffering and not-suffering go on anyway. But Charity could live as easily in paradise as she does on earth. That is what lovers know. That is Aphrodite's relation to her. Lovers are not lacking in Charity. It's just that it comes easily to them. Charity could be the Queen of Heaven. She could be Goja. She could be the Goldfish Ranisaheb. Even I could be Charity when I smile, in that instant, for that moment.

Now I can see them:

Charity and Aphrodite, goddesses off-duty,

sitting on the doorstep, enjoying the sun.

5
GODS

The gods are like monkeys. They have
pink faces and grey eyes. They sit upon
the mango trees and grin in wild surmise.

No. The gods are aristocratic.
They do not leap, they walk. They do not
walk, they stroll. They are not harried.

The gods are like gods. One or two
have imperfections, but they're undiseased.
If they die, that's extraordinary!

The mind of a twelve-year-old tries to make sense of what's on offer. Like Caliban I had gods, but they were Greek. Having been taught an alien language, I learnt how to praise alien gods. But the Christian God was a non-starter—I had been given strict instructions by my elders. And in any case the Bearded Patriarch was too implacable, too severe, too jealous and not gentle enough. Besides, Goja had told me god was in everything. Pantheism. But I didn't know the word then.

Without being conscious of it I thought of my parents and grandparents as godlike beings: they were remote, they were powerful and I loved and admired them. And they were not entirely inaccessible. Even from within the confines of a boarding school it was possible to send letters to them, provided a sufficient number of stamped envelopes had been squirreled away. And if letters are sent week after week, the gods respond. My campaign worked. I was taken away from school. But before I could see him, my father was killed when his plane crashed. I could not forgive him for dying. I thought the gods were immortal and could not be harmed. I could not believe that he was really dead or even that there was such a thing as death. Night after night, year after year, for many years, I had a recurrent dream: he hadn't died, he had run away because he didn't care any more.

I didn't know how to grieve. It was as though some bits of my brain had been blanked out. I was sent back to the American school (at my own request), and taken away again after a year and put into a different school.

At first the new school felt strange because almost everything there was Indian: the students, the food, the music, even the classical dancing. Most of the teachers were Indian as well. But the language we were taught in was English. The authorities tried to do everything in accordance with the precepts of J. Krishnamurthi, i.e. they tried to minimise authority. "Where there is fear there cannot be love." But fear does not vanish so easily, and love is not a commodity that grows on trees. Still, they tried. The Principal was a kind man who felt sorry for me. He expressed his kindness by trying to answer my questions. He had a pink face and blue eyes; his hair was not like metal, it was white. He was English.

It occurs to me that Miss M was English and Mrs C was

Scottish in a sea of Americans. Is there something about me that Americans instinctively dislike? Is it mutual? Is there some right response I refuse to give? What is it that the citizens of Rome demand? Confirmation, perhaps, when they say: "We are best. We are right. We must rule. You are wrong." I suppose this is what the family wanted of Goja, what the powerful always demand of the powerless: service with a smile.

Why did I invent gods and what use were they to me? Perhaps a child goes through the same process as a culture does when it invents a religion—in the same way that a foetus goes through the stages of evolution. Perhaps the point about gods is their superiority: "I do not want to be a god. I cannot hope to be a god, but I can make my parents and grandparents gods." Perhaps it was natural. Everyone else had made them gods—the Rajasaheb, the Ranisaheb, my mother the Akkasaheb, and my father, just plain Saheb, the high-flying, tiger-shooting pilot. Bow down and worship. Why not? And convenient. But so impossibly hard to forgive when it becomes clear that the gods are not gods, they are puny, helpless, fallible and mortal.

At the new school three "gods" were on offer. The first possible god was J. Krishnamurthi. I had no conviction he was a god, which eliminated him, since gods are dependent on their worshippers. Everyone said he was a good philosopher, and this time, since I had no instructions to the contrary when I left home, I assumed he was. He used to come to the school for a couple of months every year and lecture to us. We could ask him questions. One day I asked him, "What is Beauty?" He thought that what was behind the question was my wanting to be the sort of person who asked that sort of question; so he talked about that. But I really had wanted to know what Beauty was—that thing that stops one while the heart thuds.

Then there was the Principal. He was kind, and answered questions; but I didn't think he was a god either. And that left my father, who was dead. I suppose to me he was a god. He had qualifications: he was kind, he told stories. Often it was the same old story about the bear or the lion he had shot, but at least he told them. And since he was dead, he could be mythologised without contradiction. He reappeared in dreams—not nightmares—just cruel dreams in which he was alive. It was the waking that was cruel.

But to qualify properly, surely a god has to exist in waking life? Perhaps the gods are only the same old ghosts, the shining, unforgiven, beloved dead?

At the J. Krishnamurthi school I was less unhappy. There were more questions than lessons, and I was only there for a short time. Once again the setting was beautiful: in the south this time, a valley with green paddy fields, red earth, and a ring of small hills with enormous boulders. A telegraph pole was made out of a single slab of rock. And the trees were different from the oaks and cedars of the Himalyan foothills, there were great tamarinds and banyans and *neem* trees. There was one tree I liked particularly, a gigantic *peepal*: when the wind blew through it, its leaves sounded like muted tinsel.

It was a quiet place to be in. The nearest small town was ten miles away. Sometimes when we went for walks we'd find a sloughed-off cobra skin, paper thin and with the pattern of the scales clearly visible. Once a friend and I came across a cobra resting under a stone. It had raised its hooded head a little and was looking at us. I thought of killing it by tipping the stone over, but then I didn't—partly out of fear, partly out of respect and partly because it seemed so unnecessary. That landscape wasn't spectacularly beautiful—there were no snow-clad peaks in the distance—and it wasn't the sunburnt landscape of Western Maharashtra, which I had internalised, but it was peaceful.

Eventually, between leaving school and entering university, I stopped looking to the adults to be gods, and I stopped expecting them to make things better. But the need to idealise remained, and acknowledging that these adults were only human beings took much longer.

I left school when I was fourteen. In many ways I was raw and ignorant. When does the mind become civilised? And how is this achieved? The landscape perhaps—the slow, dripping beauty of the landscape relentlessly entering the eyes, the skin. At some point the body decides it wishes to live, the shock of death begins to wear off, and when the sky burns, so does the blood. To have energy is something. Everything perhaps, whatever one's failures. When those one loved say farewell, when they die, do they give up their energies? Do they say, "I can no more?"

At that time I was alive and physically well, however foolish, however muddled. And at about that time I discovered paradise, a sketchy paradise, a schoolgirl's paradise, but good enough.

When does the adoration of that long line of goddesses begin? With that first falling in love? Or earlier? In childhood? With the adoration of Goldfish Grandma? My grandmother's name was the name of a goddess. Almost every Hindu name is the name of a god or a goddess. Except Goja's. Was Goja not a goddess then? She's dead and she recurs. And she's acquiring stature moment by moment.

"O nightingale, nightingale,
what is a god, what is not a god?"
Is a dying father a god? Constantly
dying? Falling endlessly out of
a sky? Is a woman one loves
—preferably hopelessly—is she a god?
Images that flare—
are they gods?
O nightingale?
Why is a god? What is achieved?
And what can these godlings do for me?

It took several years before I could dissociate Christianity from that first school and read the Bible with any pleasure. It seemed to me that Jesus Christ was a likeable god. This had little to do with orthodox religion or a religious conversion. It was more an exploration of a powerful myth. That Jesus could be treated with thc same respect as any other god was clear to me. When we were little, my brothers had once brought home from their convent school a "holy picture" of Jesus Christ; and instead of being annoyed, my grandmother had stuck it in the *Devghar* (the house of the gods) together with all the other gods. Jesus could be admitted to the pantheon, and whatever he was—son of god or woman—at least he cared about what happened. Over the years his story acquired meaning for me.

It seemed to me that an Implacable God had demanded of human beings that they try to live with a degree of kindness towards the whole of creation under *circumstances that made it impossible*. But this would have been a cruel joke had it not been for Love or Charity. That is what redeemed the situation. Well, at least it made an attempt possible.

Love the Mediator said to God,
"They can't help themselves.
They are so constituted
that they have to kill in order to eat."
And God—a dazzling blankness—
did not even blink.
Love tried again:
"What is possible
is not perfection, but damage limitation.
I could teach them gentleness,
curb desire . . ."
God stayed blank,
till Love dejected,
blurted out sadly,
"I could teach them to eat what they kill."

I don't know whether I am saying that in order to survive we have to kill. I am saying that being able to love seems absurd sometimes, even foolish, certainly not prudent. But perhaps it's this very senselessness that gives Love its glory, its propensity to sacrifice, its relationship to death, its paradoxical victory. Whatever little I glimpsed of this took many years, and without Goja, and without my grandmother, I do not think it would have been possible.

6
PARADISE: ITS LOCATION

There is no comfort in this landscape:
that is its gift. It allows the clarity
of grief, and permits one just to gape
at it, but offers no possibility
that things are not as they seem, or that lies
have not been told. It casts no covering
over anything—black rock, burnt grass; it denies
nothing, not even its own harshness. Suffering?
Sometimes happens. There's nothing strange in this.
Rocks don't move, nor trees droop in sympathy.
Why should they move or droop? What is is what there is.

Can two schoolgirls call themselves partners in paradise? They wouldn't dare. But they were something. They had a name, a shape, a habitation, and they were alive. Perhaps only very young girls can inhabit paradise. They have faith; hope hasn't as yet been battered out of them, and they have the right acculturation: the gentleness of women and the near hopelessness of their love. Auden says somewhere that only lesbians make true romantic lovers. But what has romantic love to do with paradise? During a reading someone once asked, "But where is Death?" Like a fool I answered, "I do not love death. I prefer life." My preferences don't matter. Death pierces the text.

That schoolgirl of forty years ago has written to me: she has had cancer, it may recur. I reply. But the past is the past. The past is dead. In this instance I have pronounced it dead.

In subsequent narratives I said to friends, "To be a lesbian in India in those days—it's probably so even now—was so appalling, so terrible, that it was like putting one's head on the block. One risked so much for love that love had to mean everything." The conclusion to this speech was a little lame: "That is why I am so serious." Presumably I meant that I was serious about love, romantic love; but then romantics are.

If one does something illegal, disobeys the rules (sins even?), one is thrown out of paradise. The very existence of King Arthur or King Mark threatens the adulterous lovers, the very existence of society threatens the lesbian lovers, the very existence of God . . . To love is to risk death. When God threw Adam and Eve out of Paradise, they didn't die. They became mortal, able to die. Perhaps being chucked out of Paradise is not just the end of life, but the end of love. Or perhaps what it means is the corruption of both life and love, of everything good.

But Adam and Eve weren't romantic lovers. They didn't have the knowledge. They didn't know that they were living dangerously, because they didn't know the meaning of danger. They were innocent or ignorant, but they weren't romantic. To be romantic one has to know one is breaking a rule, running a risk, and all for the sake of something that matters. Lucifer possibly was a romantic.

Adolescents, particularly adolescent girls, are prime romantics in certain cultures, in certain periods . . . We weren't schoolgirls. We had finished school. We were young college students, sixteen and seventeen respectively. We fell in love, but had to work it out—how to have an affair. Literature was helpful, since we were both literary. But for lesbians?

For us danger was not around the corner, it was ever present. There were gardens in which it was possible to walk. But one day a servant saw us kiss, and reported on it. Eventually the grownups decided they could no longer ignore what was happening. Separation followed and punishment. We saw each other anyway, whenever possible. With a heady idealism we worked hard to combat tyranny. It created a state of mind that was very like paradise: everything blazed, everything roared, everything was worthwhile. If idealism is necessary to paradise, then paradise is a place of innocence. But the opposite of innocence is not guilt. It's experience. Now I see what Blake meant.

In a lesbian paradise the snake can be a man, and God is a plurality of gods, the important adults. And so it came about. But it's very confusing if you're a Hindu and live in India. My partner had an affair with an older man, a foreigner. A scandal ensued. I hadn't known about it. Eventually I was told. For me it was the shattering of Paradise, Truth, Illusion, Beauty, Faith, Hope, etcetera . . . Probably not of Charity. And the man wasn't a snake. He was only a man. Eventually they married. And there was no plurality of gods, there was only society: people who gossiped, people who were concerned, and people who were intent on their own affairs.

And yet, for me, it wasn't quite like that. For me there was the shock of understanding that reality had altered. I remember staring at the grass, at the trees. That was when the landscape helped. It absorbed emotion. The lion-coloured grass was still lion-coloured. The *babul* tree with its silver thorns, and tough, black trunk, still rose from the ground. The landscape was still strewn with round black stones, the concentric rings of lava bubbles could still be traced in the volcanic rocks. The light was still harsh, the black shadows were very black, the brightness was still bright. And the great banyans occupied space. I knew that it was possible to bleed into that landscape, to live in it, to die in it. Others had. I knew that the landscape could absorb grief, though there was a dark space, which even the landscape could not occupy. Perhaps that dark space was the awareness of betrayal, or of mortality perhaps. End of paradise.

She had not had the heart to tell me how things stood. Or perhaps she lacked the courage. And therefore I found out by chance. But I suppose, however I had found out, this sort of knowledge is always difficult.

I've just understood: Paradise isn't a different place, a different landscape. It was earth that fell, and did not fall. The earth absorbed everything: all the death to come, the dripping blood. That is why the earth is so lovely sometimes: it is paradise, and it is fallen. And that is why we want to live—because we inhabit paradise.

What happens to adolescents? What do they suffer? They grow up. Some decide that to cease looking for paradise is to grow up. Others decide that to start looking for a possible paradise, a circumscribed paradise, that's to grow up. They compromise. They keep looking for paradise—paradise was the only thing worth having. They decide that paradise is out there somewhere. Or they decide that paradise has got to be here on earth. They decide—poor things, what do they decide? In their confusion they've experienced a heightened reality, but whether it's a glimpse of something better or only an illusion, isn't clear.

Romantic lovers aren't concerned with Love in the sense of Charity. Charity is only needed when Paradise is lost. Is she the daughter of suffering? I would have preferred it had she been the daughter of joy. Pleasure and Joy are Psyche's children. It's a great thing to have given the world at least one good myth —lucky Apuleius. My mind is a hodgepodge of Greek myth, Hindu experience and Christian words; but I have understood that Charity is neither the daughter of suffering, nor of joy. She has a human face. Blake understood it all along.

As students it was our ignorance that made us think we could have a happy ending. Or perhaps we believed what we wanted to believe. We laughed at our professors, made silly jokes, defied our families, and thought our thoughts. We lost a year. Then we pulled ourselves together, and worked at our studies with a furious practicality. The idea was that I would somehow enter the Administrative Service, by sheer hard work I would do well in the competitive exam and get selected even though it was very difficult. And then we would be independent and live happily together like any ordinary couple! The romantic dream was a very banal one. What distinguished it was that in India it was impossible.

Well, she did get married, and I did get selected for the Administrative Service. I had gone on working mechanically, though the happy ending had been blown out of existence. The family was delighted I had been selected for the IAS, and I was pleased rather than otherwise. I thought having a job other people coveted would give me some respect and independence.

A love affair is an oasis. It punctuates ordinary life with glimpses of paradise. And that is why people sometimes honour their old loves: they remember that at one time in their arms there was ecstasy. But the blazing, roaring earthly paradise of young lovers is not the home of Charity, though she can visit there. But then she can visit anywhere because she is kind.

7
LEAVING

I said to Charity,
"You beam at seedlings growing indoors
which your care and affection nourished,
and take no thought for the bitter spring
when some will thrive and the rest perish."
But Charity said,
"Damn you, sweetie. If death were to determine
anything, then the whole world journeying
sorrowfully over the falls would die
of neglect precisely because it was already dying!"

I was old enough to feel grief this time. The landscape didn't change, no veil was lifted or drawn; but it had altered. During this period while I was going through my own disillusionment, I was only marginally aware that other people also inhabited the landscape. And I understood only in a distant fashion that the landscape had also absorbed their loss and their pain. But conditions in India are such that even I had noticed that many of the people looked resigned. And this look of resignation was there in the eyes of cyclists and of pedestrians, of people driving bullock carts and of people standing still. It was there in the eyes of the women as well as the men, and in the eyes of people in towns and cities and also in villages. And it troubled me, because this was Western Maharashtra. This was my landscape and these were my people: I didn't want them distinguished by the lines of defeat stamped on their foreheads. Usually there was less anxiety in the eyes of villagers—perhaps because they had no hope at all of effecting change. But the look was there: time and life had worn them too fast, too soon.

"Why should they be resigned?" I thought, "While there's energy, there's life, there's blood." But I was relatively rich. If I had asked, perhaps they'd have said, "That's the problem. There isn't energy, life and blood. Those are the privileges of the rich." But I didn't ask.

The Moral Imperative said, "Thou shalt not exploit other people and feed off their flesh." To be born is not a birthright, but once born, to be allowed to grow and live, and if at all possible, to be happy, surely these things should be inalienable. Why not? Why snigger at the Americans for wanting to pursue happiness?

It was the discrepancy between the poor and the rich that felt so wrong, not just the poverty. The gap was so vast that it seemed to imply there was no kinship between them, that they were two different species. And underneath all this was the appalling knowledge that we were not two different species: what was being done, we were doing to ourselves.

In the West the gap between the rich and the poor is increasing again. For a while they improved the lot of their poor, but surely this was done at the expense of their colonies. Presumably, at the height of Empire, any Englishman, however foolish, however stupid, however rapacious, or however well-meaning, could go out there somewhere and do well for himself, and be a bit of a ruler for a while. And after the colonies went, much could be done to maintain prosperity by maintaining an economic stranglehold: "We'll buy your raw materials cheap. You buy our manufactured goods at an enormous price."

Some time ago on the television news there were pictures of the poor in Albania literally scavenging on the rubbish heaps. As I watched I wondered whether the fact that they were European made the sight seem particularly dreadful. (The Albanian children picking through garbage made me think of my own condition: if I am bruised, at least I fall on sweet-smelling earth.) Some months later viewers were told that the television coverage had been set up by a photographer: he had paid them to scavenge. But then that too proves something.

For as long as I can remember, the family—my mother's family; of my father's family there was little left—had been declining steadily. The Princely States had been merged. Inflation had eaten into the privy purse, which the government had decreased anyway. And because my grandfather had joined the Congress Party, he had incurred election expenses. His lands, though distributed between his sons and daughter, had been greatly reduced. Times had changed: feudalism had given way to capitalism. And perhaps because of the caste system, the family hadn't coped very well. (It was like asking Klingons to behave like Ferengi, though I suspect that clever Klingons are part Ferengi anyway, and vice versa.)

Is there that much difference between the old aristocracy and the new plutocracy? Both are exploitative. Both offer protection of sorts—on their terms—*from themselves!*—and when it suits them.

At times, as I was growing up, I babbled idealism at members of the family: of course everyone should be looked after, of course communism was a good thing, of course a leper should be picked up and cherished. I had arguments with my grandfather, the Raja, who had metamorphosed into a minister in the Bombay cabinet. He was patient and "explained things properly". I suppose the idea was that my idealism and his patience reflected well on both of us. It didn't do much for anyone else, except perhaps that through his example I learnt never to be rude to the poor. (No doubt the poor were duly impressed!)

Perhaps I also learnt a degree of generosity, though such generosity is treacherous. It is so easy, so tempting, "to fix up things" for a poor individual with a flick of the pen. It generates notions of grandeur, and reinforces images of a glittering nobility magnificently obliging the ignoble poor. There are worse things, but this is an unlovely spectacle.

There were times when the horror penetrated. One day my mother lined up her four children, my sister, my brothers and me, and told us we were escapists, lotus eaters all, unwilling to face anything unpleasant. She said she had taken a servant to the doctor that day. Someone had vomited on the doctor's doorstep, and she had seen a beggar woman eat up the vomit. We were appalled. I asked myself what I was supposed to do? Become a social worker? I didn't want to be a social worker. And in my mind I lashed back at my mother: was a petulant princess any better?

I did nothing. The poor were shadows. *(Even though they were everywhere?)* They were functions when encountered in the form of servants. I was absorbed in my own dream. Perhaps young people always are. I wanted to be someone, do something. Be a mathematician perhaps, or a writer? No, someone that others would bow down to—a member of the glittering Civil Service with which the British had ruled India. I wanted to be someone in my own right. Not the Rajasaheb's granddaughter, nor the test pilot's gosling. (Why gosling? Neither swan nor duck, is that what I mean?) I didn't know then that no one is someone in their own right. Recognition requires another pair of eyes.

As I write death once again enters the text. An interruption? How can Death be an interruption? One of my aunts this time, my favourite. When I first met her, I was only thirteen or fourteen. To my barbarous schoolgirl mind, her youth offered a first understanding of spring. She was like a young tree. Now she has faded away, I too am getting older.

> When the light falls so flatly on the sea
> that the motion of the waves seems sluggish,
> and the water itself lifeless, then we know
> that this is the beach where it all ends,
> no, where it ends for us, while you,
> with a nod and a smile, walk into that sea
> as though it were just another day.

She was a most loving woman, even when she knew that Death was nearby, was standing there, waiting. Now when people are loving, I think to myself, "As children they must have been loved." This is not to lessen their grace, but to remind myself how easily we get damaged.

* * *

It so happened that I did well in the civil service exam, got selected and became "someone". I did indeed. Everyone said so. If enough people say something happened, then it did happen. That's corroboration! Testimony relies on language. And sanity relies on consensus. Amazing. It's in this sense that I became "someone". But surely I existed before? The knowledge that with or without recognition one continues to live was what sustained me when I was stripped of my identity years later. Whether or not anyone is watching, the rain rains down, water is sweet. But at the time they—the contiguous world—all assured me I had become someone: I had become an officer in the Indian Administrative Service.

I was not bowed down to and worshipped, but I was bowed down to. I was posted to my home state, and I saw that look of resignation again in the eyes of the people I was supposed to serve. What went on was both real and unreal. I knew very little, I tried to do my job and that was about it. Others about me, especially below me, who had put in long years of service, must have known I knew very little, and yet, it was "Yes, Your Honour", "No, Your Honour", and "We all stand up, and we all fall down." They must have known that much of the charade—theirs as well as mine—was hollow. And the poor must have known it too—the poor who were strangled and thwarted and bullied by the administration.

It shames me that I enjoyed my status: people rising when I entered an office, the police springing to attention and presenting arms when I visited a subdivision. But what shamed me even then to the point of being hurtful was gratitude from the poor for doing my work. They were grateful because although I had the power, I did not harm or hinder.

Perhaps the realistic assessment of power is realism. But its unrealistic assessment can give power to those to whom it's attributed. Hype! When they said, "Ji Maharaj" to my grandparents, and to their children and to their grandchildren, that was hype—necessary hype from the point of view of the powerful—because as long as it was maintained or could be maintained, the king continued to be King and the emperor to be Emperor, and the adulation and admiration is and was *(and ever shall be world without end?)* real.

Now when I have very little power I have at last understood something about power. I think some sort of conditioning went on—for humanists and "civilised" people and especially for women—that prohibited any serious thinking about power. It would not have been comfortable.

What little power I had I used to do my job. I settled land cases speedily. I answered letters rapidly. I went on tour. I visited villages. I regulated elections honestly. I did not take bribes. And I did not bully anyone. It is perhaps true that being my grandfather's granddaughter I could afford to be honest. Nobody dared to bully me, and I did not actually need to take bribes. But to fail to do evil is hardly to do good.

If all I did was fail to do evil, it's not surprising that after a few years I went abroad and quit the Administrative Service. I had begun to find it tedious. A better person might have stayed on—or a worse person. In addition I was seriously in love with a dear friend—I shall call her Sahali. She had already gone abroad and it seemed sensible to follow. By then it was clear that in India it would not be possible for two women, who loved one another, to live honourably together. There was another reason for going abroad. The English language had colonised my brain, but I had never seen the reality behind the words. I was in my mid-twenties and had written a little and published a little; but more and more I was beginning to think that if I worked hard I could some day become a really good writer. I wanted to look at the reality behind the words in order to use the words better.

I took leave of Goja and my grandmother and the rest of the family and set off for the States. I did not tell them that I did not mean to return. I had study leave from the Government of India and a research assistantship at a Midwestern university to do a Master's in public administration. I did the Master's, resigned from the Administrative Service, and went to Canada where I did my doctorate in English Literature and then taught there for many years—almost as many as I had lived in India before leaving for the West.

Now, as I try to put together the two halves of my experience, I live in the country in England with my partner. This, once again, is an entirely different landscape—sometimes it's like living inside an emerald. If I had told Goja and my grandmother all those years ago that I did not mean to return, it would not have been true. I have returned year after year for the past thirty years. And then I have returned again and again year after year to the West like some silly goose or determined salmon. In the course of those years both Goja and my grandmother have died. I did not mean to abandon them. I could not.

I had thought once that I felt most at home in a plane in midair; but that isn't true. I belong to India and to the West. Both belong to me and both reject me. I have to make sense of what has been and what there is.

PART II

FROM COLD CANADA

8
UNREASONABLE THINGS

I had entered a new world and I had escaped the family, but I was too frightened to enjoy the freedom of near invisibility. My being invisible allowed truck drivers to run me over. Not that they did. Shop assistants could forget I was waiting. This did happen. And ignorant Americans could patronise me. And this happened too sometimes. In a way they did notice me. I was both invisible and conspicuous. In their eyes—even when I was wearing a beautiful sari—I had on a white garment which had written on it in large black letters: FOREIGN / EXOTIC / THIRD WORLD / NEEDY—whichever word their mind's eye was able to read.

That first year was spent in a small American town doing a Master's in public administration. One day a man stopped me in the street: "Excuse me, sir, what strange garment is that you're wearing?" I do not look masculine and I do not look American. Perhaps that was the point. In order to be recognised I had to look either like a white man or like something appertaining to one: a white woman or a white child. It took me a while to understand that I was being subjected to ethnocentric racism. I wasn't expecting it. I thought I looked normal and I thought they did too. I had, after all, grown up with these people in that school long ago in the Himalayan foothills.

Soon after I got there a fellow student invited me home for the Thanksgiving weekend. I was pleased to be asked and went along happily, but without being aware of it, I made the wrong assumptions. Her parents spoke English and I thought that meant they had had a certain education. The person who invited me had told me her father worked in a car factory and was of Polish extraction, but that meant nothing to me. It was not that I was free of prejudgements, it was just that my prejudices belonged to a different country.

What happened next was sad and funny, and for a few years it traumatised me. I vowed that I would work with these people, meaning Westerners, talk with these people, eat with these people, but that I would never again stay with these people because they had such peculiar manners and didn't seem to be able to behave properly!

My fellow student's father happened to be watching television when we entered their house. "Look, look, see, see," he said (or the equivalent) pointing to the screen. "Here are tigers and lions. Do you have tigers and lions in India?"

I thought this was a form of social conversation. I was willing to try it. "Yes," I replied politely.

"No, no," he said, "you don't have lions in India. It's in Africa they have lions and tigers."

"Well, on the whole you're right," I told him diffidently, remembering that respect for one's elders was important and he was older than me. "There's only one place in India—the Gir forest—where we do have lions."

I didn't tell him there were no tigers in Africa.

He then said, "There are no lions in India."

I didn't say anything.

Next he informed me that my teeth were very white. I decided this was more social conversation of a peculiar sort.

"Actually, they're not," I responded conversationally. "I had some fillings done just before I left India, and the dentist showed me how carefully he had to match the enamel to get the shade exactly right. No one's teeth are absolutely white." I had found this interesting and thought that it might interest him. I didn't realise until much much later that he had meant my teeth were white in contrast with my skin.

The non sequiturs and mismatched meanings continued all weekend. I flooded their bathroom when I had a shower because I forgot that the bathroom wasn't completely tiled and that one didn't splash water as one did in India. They were nice about it and helped me mop it up. Then they suggested that I phone my family all the way in India because it was Thanksgiving. When I explained that in India we didn't celebrate Thanksgiving, they were hurt and puzzled and a little disapproving.

It was like being Alice in Wonderland. Strange and aggressive creatures kept insisting they were right; and any experience I had, which might have helped, somehow never applied properly.

But I wasn't Alice and I wasn't in a book. In the course of that year I began to understand the full extent of the racism and the ethnocentricity. I was hurt and powerless and very sorry for myself. I became quick to take offence and armed myself with a verbal knife. The weapons that I was best at using were sarcasm and irony. These I had seen in action and had learnt from the family. But I found that more often than not my carefully crafted shafts were lost on the Americans. That there was a deeper and even more subtle irony in all this I completely failed to see.

I was infuriated by what I thought of as their wilful stupidity. I vowed that if they patronised me, I'd patronise them back ten times over! I muttered darkly that I had forgotten more about snobbery than they had ever learnt! And since I hadn't yet resigned from the Administrative Service, I found it particularly galling that these Americans didn't know—or if they knew, they didn't care—what the IAS was! Nor had they ever heard of the princely states, never mind the Rajasaheb or the Ranisaheb! And then I'd feel ashamed. And when I had earned ten dollars for cleaning someone's floors, I'd feel proud of myself for having done "servant's work" without complaining.

Goja, forgive me. I was young and foolish.

I decided that of the different kinds of stupidity, it was the impenetrable stupidity of the Americans that was the most unappealing. I understand now that there was nothing that belonged to a particular nationality about what it was that hurt me. This wilful, unprocessed, unameliorated ignorance I'm calling stupidity is a function of power. The powerful are stupid. Citizens of Rome are stupid in relation to the rest of the world. Human beings are stupid in relation to the rest of creation, masters are stupid in relation to servants, men in relation to women, adults in relation to children, the rich in relation to the poor . . .

In my letters home and on my first trip back I said little or nothing about what was happening to me. I was afraid that the family would laugh and say it served me right. (The warrior caste is not known for its kindness.) And worse than that, they'd be contemptuous of me. Only someone very contemptible would choose to live where they were being humiliated. I should never have gone abroad. I certainly shouldn't have stayed. If bad things happened, that was too bad. It was what I deserved for deserting the family, and for throwing away a career in the civil service that would have reflected well on everybody. As a poor student in North America I wasn't much use to anybody.

I remember that Goja asked me how I was getting on. She found it hard to believe that over there people were expected to do their own washing, cook their own dinners, sweep their own floors. Did I really do all that? She sounded incredulous and a little concerned. I tried to explain about vacuum cleaners. It was hopeless. She found it hard to understand or to credit. But I like to remember sitting on the steps and talking with her. At least we had that bit of time. Goldie, my grandmother—I mean no disrespect—also asked me about life in America, but she had been to the States herself twenty years before me and had had a much grander time. There wasn't much point in saying anything. But now it's different. Now I'd like to explain, bridge the two worlds, say some of the things that were left unsaid and arrive at some understanding between them and me.

In the West, as a person of no importance, I was unlikely to cause a scandal. And there was no family there whose glory I could tarnish. What I did or who I was didn't matter, because I didn't matter. I was a student again, and had no family and no background. I was nobody. That was freedom of a sort. After that first year my dear friend and I, the one I've called Sahali, managed to get admission and a little money at the same university. I moved to Canada and we lived together as impoverished students. For a time we were happy. And because in Canada we lived in Montreal, a cosmopolitan city, rather than in a small town, the prejudices and the parochialism were less extreme. Besides, the Canadians seemed far less insistent on making us reflect their own reality than the Americans had been.

In spite of being treated like a person of no account, indeed in spite of being a person of no account—that was what was hard—I had not returned to the family. Instead I resigned from the Administrative Service and managed to get a teaching assistantship in order to do a doctorate in English. It was a rejection of my family. It was a bid for freedom. It was an irresponsible action. It was the price I paid for love. Many descriptions are possible. I don't think Goja or Goldie would have seen it quite like that.

Perhaps they'd have said that I wanted to be a much loved member of a large family *and* I wanted my freedom. Perhaps they'd have said that I wanted to be someone important in society, someone who was respected, *and* I wanted to be who I wanted to be. And perhaps they'd have added that this was very unreasonable of me. If at the time I had been able to say that wanting to be a good poet, and being allowed to live honourably as a lesbian were not unreasonable things, they would have been amazed, even horrified. They would have said, "Yes, they *are* unreasonable things." And I would have had to agree. Being a poet is hardly an occupation one can write on a passport, and as for being lesbian—well, that was horrid. Everyone said so—it was a horrid and unmentionable thing. Perhaps that was why during their lifetimes I never had the nerve to say anything to them. But now? Goja? Goldie? I would like if possible to make my peace.

It may be that behind the labels—poet, lesbian, artist, bohemian, poor person, student—I was guilty of a more fundamental crime: I was unwilling to serve the family and to conform to society. There was an implicit bargain, and if I wasn't keeping my side of it, then the family and society weren't able to keep their side of it. I had thrown in my lot with the West; very well then, let the West look after me.

There was, however, a turning point when I very nearly returned to India even though I no longer had a job and would have been wholly dependent on the family. Sahali and I were living in a small apartment near the university. It was an ordinary winter's day: there was snow on the ground, slush in the streets, and clean white snow lay on the upper slopes of the branches, while intensely black shadows slid along the underside. It was bitterly cold and the sun was shining. I had nearly finished my dissertation on Pound's *Cantos*. Everything was going well, and suddenly it all meant nothing. Sahali informed me that she was not a lesbian, that she did not wish to continue in the relationship and that by having "made her" participate in the relationship I had mutilated her. It left me feeling as though a part of my brain had been torn out of me. There were broken blood vessels, loose connections, and veins and nerve ends that suddenly led nowhere. It took time to heal.

I finished my doctorate, applied for a job, got a job and then spent the next seventeen years or so in Toronto teaching English Literature and Canadian poetry. I'm not altogether sure why I didn't return to India. It was not because I thought that my existence in the West was likely to be completely trouble-free. The West had its own brand of homophobia and its own kind of sexism, and it had racism as well. I had no family in the West, no network of connections. The Canadians hadn't actually asked me to come or begged me to stay. From their point of view they could have done without me. It's true that I scored well enough on their points system and that they hadn't had the expense of my early education. And I could argue that they had benefited from the "brain drain", but there wasn't really much point to such arguments. What was worth noting was that I found it necessary to justify myself. It was clear to me that in that context I was hardly mainstream. Reality was what they said it was, not what I said it was or could be or might have been.

Still, I wasn't altogether helpless. Their version of who I really was had to deal with my version of who I really was. It was the same for them. There were multiple realities. They made patterns, and they could be manipulated. I was learning

When I arrived in Toronto I had a few cardboard boxes with odds and ends and a suitcase full of clothes. I had a job, and I had some skills. But I had no past, no history and no human framework supporting me. I felt stripped. What was strange though was that in some ways I quite liked this. Having a little money made a difference. As students we had had very little money, and not having to worry about the rent and the groceries helped enormously. And just having a job gave me some status. When I arrived in Toronto I was in bad shape, and also a little frightened, but in spite of this there was a sensation of freedom. It tasted and smelt like cold Canada. It had the smell of snow and it was exhilarating. After all, I had a few weapons now. Not just the job and the money, but language and understanding. I was beginning to learn how to use language, and that mediated everything.

I had written my doctoral dissertation on Pound's *Cantos* because I had wanted to learn a poet's skills by studying him. And I had worked hard. I thought about the *Cantos* as I walked down the street. I even dreamed about them sometimes. When I had finished, I resolved to work at least as hard at my own writing.

The most important thing about my encounter with the West was the English language. It took me several years and required my politicisation to understand how language had power over power itself. Over the years, language mediated everything: my struggle with powerlessness and loss of identity, my understanding of who defined whom and how effectively, and my need to work out what really mattered and somehow to say it. What worried and delighted me at this time was how language cloaked, altered and even fashioned reality, how there were multiple realities, and how it was possible to juxtapose these so that they resonated and shimmered and multiplied meaning.

9

ENCHANTED FORESTS

When I first came to North America I had felt confident about my ability to deal with the Americans and Canadians. I knew about them. I knew their language, *and then I discovered I didn't!* I understood the words, but not the context. I understood the words, but I understood them differently. "Lift" did not mean "elevator," because they did not know that was what it meant. What was annoying was that they did not choose to know. All yellow flowers which looked like stars against a green backdrop were not daffodils, they were more likely to be dandelions. I was not an Indian, their indigenous peoples were . . . I was not myself?

In India the West had been composed of words, English words. It's not surprising then that entering the States, and then a year later Canada, was like entering a forest of words. Often these places were more like woods, orchards, thickets . . . "Out of this wood do not desire to go . . ." Why? What does it mean? And why weren't there notices keeping people out? *(Oh there were!)* But I felt easy in the enchanted forests. I liked it there. Dragons, demons, dazzlers—whatever the forest had to offer was fine. These were familiar things. I could handle them. No problem. The inside of my head could contain any number of enchanted forests, and I liked walking about inside my head.

It was the connection between these enchanted forests and the "real" Canadian trees that presented difficulties. The correspondence between the words and the reality or even my own experience wasn't straightforward. "Beech", "oak", "maple"—fine, no problem there. These were words in English. And if the words were used, they reliably conjured English trees. Well, there was sometimes a problem: these were Canadian trees that the words were supposed to conjure. Canadian poets had to deal with that. Was I not a Canadian poet? Well . . . My own problem was slightly different. It had to do with waking and sleeping.

At the time I rented a flat on the top floor of a house on a quiet street, and like most streets this particular one had trees growing along it. Sometimes the trees along the streets were silver birches, sometimes they were chestnuts; these particular ones happened to be maples. When I looked through the windows in the summer, I could see the branches of the trees and the leaves. And when I woke up in the morning the leaves were there. *My difficulty was that they were the wrong shape.*

All night long I dreamed about what was inside my head. I dreamed about the reality that I had known, I dreamed about India. The leaves of the tree should have been *neem* leaves, the delicate, curved, serrated *neem* leaves, not large, floppy maple ones. All night long I had been sleeping under a *neem* tree. It was strange to wake up in the pale Canadian light to a totally different landscape. Sometimes I would have to lie there for a second or two and try to remember not just where I was, but who I was. At first it was a little frightening, but I got used to it. I was fairly sure that if I waited for a second or two, memory would come back. I would know who I was supposed to be and would get on with whatever it was I was supposed to be doing.

But it was disturbing that I could not see the shape of the leaves properly, that I could not like them for being themselves. That took much longer. It took a long time.

If I thought of the leaves as words, then I was all right. Words could be difficult, recalcitrant; but I could deal with words. It was my training, my craft. It was the thing on which I was spending my time. I could—given enough practice and time—be a maker of trees. An arranger. I wanted to be a good poet. And it would have to be in English. My Marathi wasn't good enough. I thought if only I could see each word, each leaf, with greater and greater clarity, and somehow focus on the shifting patterns of the leaves, see clearly, always see clearly, then there would be such wealth! Once I got the hang of it, such prowess! I could redesign the landscape! Or I could just gape at it. Or both! It seemed to me that there was, is and shall be such splendour, such a world of splendour from the ghost gums of Australia to the ash tree Yggdrasil. It seemed to me that in paradise they did not name the trees, they recited their names. "Paradise" was a word. "Forest" was a word. The leaves were words. They allowed me to enter an enchanted forest. They were the forest. How could it be otherwise? The English language had colonised my mind.

But the ghost gums of Australia and the ash tree Yggdrasil did not grow in Canada, nor in India either. And whatever the power of mythical or exotic trees, robed in splendour, rooted in earth and spreading their branches among the heavens, there was something to be said for the ordinary old tree growing by the wayside. I could look at it, feel its bark, smell its leaves, and even bang my head against it if that was what I felt like.

Sometimes I couldn't see the trees for the leaves, until I crashed straight into a tree. And sometimes I could see all right, but all the other denizens of the forest insisted I couldn't. Because, of course, I was not the sole inhabitant of this forest. Other people lived there, bumped into me, contradicted me, colluded with me. It's not just young romantics and aspiring poets who inhabit enchanted forests. Everyone does. Hard rock and solid trees are mediated by words. *Where one is* is a word. *Who one is* is a word—Indian, lesbian, poet, Hindu, donkey, monkey, dying animal . . . And much of one's life is just a matter of exploring words to see which ones fit comfortably, and in which forest of words one might live and breathe.

The enchanted forest and the real forest are not distinct. The one fits over the other. That is why it's so easy to get confused, to lose one's way, to be misled by strangers who offer directions with complete conviction. And there are complications, there are natives who say that they are not natives. And still others who point out that the forest itself has been completely transplanted, that the forest itself is not native . . . Some of the Canadian trees originally grew on Himalayan slopes. I think I found the discomfort of the English-speaking Canadians comforting. I liked their understanding that things were not quite as they seemed.

One day I did crash into a tree. We had gone cross-country skiing. This is a solitary occupation even with friends. The evergreen trees were laden with snow—mostly spruce and fir. The snow had outlined them with such care. In these woods no birds sang because there were no birds. They had all gone south except for a few snow sparrows. I am not certain that is their right name. I lost control on a gentle slope and crashed into a tree. Perhaps it was a beech or an oak. I could make it up.

I know that it was not an elm. Most of the elm trees caught a disease and they're nearly all gone.

It's strange to have had the experience, but to have lost the word. And sometimes there are words, but no experience attaches to them, or they're not understood.

The split between sleeping and waking, night and day, literature and life, India and Canada, between things and their name, words and their meaning, was auditory as well as visual.

Goja and Goldie and my grandfather sometimes would sit like hecklers in a gallery and comment loudly on what was going on inside my head. And sometimes they would ignore what was going on—it was my head after all, I was centre-stage—and chat among themselves. If they got me into trouble, they would just laugh. For example, it was because of their training, that I would spring to my feet when elderly gentlemen walked into a room, and then I would have to pretend that I had merely risen to get some coffee . . . And sometimes Goja and Goldie (perched there like two wise birds in the rafters of my mind) would scold and insist that I keep quiet and behave myself. Once a foolish young woman invited me to dinner at an expensive restaurant. Then she patronised me by saying she knew Indians were poor and she therefore hoped I hadn't been overwhelmed. Goja and Goldie, cackling up there inside my head, wouldn't allow me to say anything back, not even when she started watching my knives and forks. In the end I got cross. I was confused about why it wasn't proper to say anything back. I got my revenge by eating up my dinner with toothpicks, but it was on Goja and Goldie that I got my revenge, not on the young woman, I didn't care about her. I was playing to the gallery in which *they* sat.

Over the years they all died: first Goja, then my grandfather, then Goldie; but since I wasn't with them anyway they didn't change very much inside my head. It was only when I returned to India on the annual visits that I missed their physical presence. Absent voices and ghostly voices aren't very different, especially when they're not absent.

I cared about what *they* thought. What the people about me thought mattered much less. Perhaps that's why eventually it was relatively easy to "come out" in the West. To relative strangers I could say, "Yes, I'm a lesbian. So what?" But it troubled me that I couldn't say it to the people I loved. Goja and Goldie, you are inside my mind so you can read what's there, but there is a difference between the living and the dead, between actually saying something and taking it as read.

Goja? Goldie? I want so much to join the two halves of my existence. For years now I've told fabulous tales to the West. And they've all been translations of a sensibility formed by what it was like growing up in India, by growing up with the two of you. Why wouldn't you let me tell you about what it was like trying to grow further in cold Canada, in that forest of words, with the two of you missing and yet always there? For a long time while you were alive, I tried to keep my books out of India so that you would never know, so that there would be no scandal—you would not have to be ashamed and so that I could continue to return year after year without too much difficulty or distress. But this account I'm now writing is for you *and* for the West. It's Janus-faced. I want to bridge my two worlds so that at last there might be the possibility of reconciliation, and if not reconciliation, then at least a degree of straightforwardness.

There are so many things I want to tell you about. The West wasn't a country of no return. Every time I left for the West, I didn't die. An impermeable pane of glass didn't suddenly come between us. I carried you with me all the time.

It's not reasonable or honest for me to say that Canada was merely an enchanted forest, or that pink people with metallic hair were imaginary creatures straight out of story books. Some of them became my friends and lovers. The West is more than a region of words. It's part of the planet. Underneath my feet there was real mud or snow or slush, depending on the season. And if all these things were also words, then the words were part of a lived life.

If I think back slowly to that earlier time, I could say as Atwood said of Susanna Moodie: "I am a word in a foreign language." Has the word "Suniti" become more acceptable? Does it fit into the West? Has the world changed? I am like a bone singing on the beach: "Has the weather smoothed me? Am I sea-changed?" Everything assimilates to everything else because it must. There's painful erosion and forced adjustment.

How can I deny that I have changed? In some ways I have become a part of the West. It was inevitable. The landscapes entered my eyes and the climate weathered my skin. But I did not betray you. I did not cease to be who I had once been. Nor did I cease to love you. I wanted to share with you what it was like, but you never came and I could not speak. There was too much to say that was forbidden.

Surely it's time? I want to tell you about Paramour, a woman I loved who was both flesh and blood and an enchantress. She dominated everything. And I want to tell you about how in the West I was sometimes hurt and humiliated without being afraid of your contempt for me. It wasn't Faith, Hope and Charity I was concerned with then, but sex, power and language. And you can't draw back and say that these things have little or nothing to do with you. They were the girders that bridged two worlds. If your charge against me is that I went away, then at least try to understand why I went away and what it was like. There are charges against you that you have to answer. And then perhaps we might find Charity.

We could sit like three crows on top of an oak tree, or we could sit on a hill in a familiar landscape among round black stones and silver thorn trees. In the past I've used words to cloak me and clothe me, I've hidden in the forest like the fawn or Alice. Goja? Goldie? *Don't you understand that I've hidden from you?* It's time we told each other stories about both the West and the East.

10
THE FABLED WEST

And because it's time, you in the West, even my friends, even my partner, you may eavesdrop if you like, look over my shoulder, snigger with horror and shock if you must; but suppress expostulation and suppress the need to explain yourselves and set me right. You see, I am now explaining the Fabulous West to the Mysterious East; you understand only the half of what I'm doing.

To whom precisely are you explaining these things?

I am explaining them to Goldfish Ranisaheb and Goja Bai.

But they're dead.

Yes, well, the dead are disinterested—clearly.

Why not stick to the present?

Your prime time ain't my prime time. Besides, we are straddling both time and space over half a century.

If I concentrate, it's easy enough to summon them. Goldfish Grandma is in a green sari, and Goja is wearing a navy blue one, which is nine yards long. It has a maroon border and is tucked up between her legs. I wonder if it's comfortable. *All the better to work with.* Goja winks. Did she really wink? That one-eyed look is hard to read sometimes.

The three of us are sitting on a hilltop. I begin talking: "In the West nobody sleeps on the streets. They live in houses or flats and almost everyone has a comfortable bed. You say that's not so. Fifty years ago you were in New York and saw one or two people who looked as though they might not have slept in a comfortable bed? Yes. Well. You're right, there are people who sleep rough, but not on the same scale as our people here. And anyway you were in America, whereas I was mostly in Canada. It's colder there."

Goldie shrugs. "That's why they don't sleep outdoors. In the cold they'd die."

Goja wants to know whether Canada is different from America.

"Well, they are different, they want to be different . . ." I break off. Goja looks politely uncomprehending, and Goldie is beginning to look bored. "The main difference," I tell Goja quickly, "is that in relation to America Canada is powerless." Goja nods. It makes sense.

I turn to Goldie. "In the West," I inform her, "there's freedom for women. There you could have been a Queen in your own right like Queen Elizabeth."

"What about me?" enquires Goja.

"Not in her own right," retorts Goldie. "She was her father's daughter, her uncle's niece."

I wish she wasn't so well informed. I try again: "In the West, the gap between the rich and the poor is not so great."

"I may be dead," Goldie remarks, "but I'm still *au courant*. I can read the papers. The gap exists, and it's widening."

Goja nods vigorously.

In despair I make a radical suggestion.

"If you are *au courant*, if you can read the papers, will you sit beside me, be fellow writers, and shall we address somebody else?"

"No, no," Goja replies, "you explain yourself to us. You do the talking. You do the writing. It's all fine. Tell us about your sexual exploits."

"What?! But that's scandalous!"

"What is scandalous?" enquires Goldie.

" A granddaughter telling her grandmothers about sex."

"So you've co-opted Goja as a grandmother then?" Goldie enquires.

"We are not characters," I remind them solemnly. "I am the omnipotent narrator, and you are the hypothetical audience."

"If you're so omnipotent, how does it matter who we are?" Goja mutters.

"I meant omniscient. But I can only say what you are able to know. It matters who you are."

"Well, I don't speak English," says Goja.

"I do," puts in Goldie, "but my Marathi is much, much better. Do this half of the book in Marathi. That will solve your problem."

"I can't."

"Why not?"

"It won't sell."

"Well, that's your problem. Who you're selling to, not who you're talking to—that's the question you ought to address."

"Goldie, you're an aristocrat, not a plutocrat. How do you know so much about selling?"

"I'm clever."

"Goja, I can't write in Marathi. You know that. My Marathi isn't good enough."

"Well, I can't read English. You know that."

"Just do it badly in bad Marathi," Goldie suggests. "Then translate. It might solve your problem."

I pick a topic I think will interest them, take a deep breath and do what she says. "Those people's children are fairer and taller than our people's children. Perhaps they are giving better meals. Gandhiji said one time it is because they eat meat, that is why. If our children were as tall and fair as theirs are, then it would have been so much good. However, whatever is happening, ours are cleverer."

Goldie cuts in sharply, "We belong to the warrior caste and do eat meat if we wish to. That I don't eat meat is a personal preference. As for my children and grandchildren they're quite as good-looking as anyone else's. That includes you. Moreover I really don't see why you have to translate what could have been perfectly good Marathi, even on your part, into some extraordinary language which is neither gibberish nor English, but which does seem to have tangled itself hopelessly in its own syntax. If you don't say something sensible soon, we'll go away and amuse ourselves."

"All right." I try to think of an amusing story. "One day one of your grandchildren—not me, one of the tiny ones, one of the last—asked her mother where I lived, and her mother opened the freezer compartment of the refrigerator and said, 'That is where.'" As I tell it, I realise that I don't find this story particularly funny.

My grandmother snorts. "That's an old story. I've heard it you know. I prefer the one about your mother in the Canadian winter, chewing *paan*—"

"Yes," I interrupt enthusiastically, "while the natives exclaim, 'Look, look, see, see Indian princess spitting rubies!'" I glance at Goja and explain that the point of the story is that it's so cold that the *paan* freezes when she spits it out and the "natives" are so silly they . . . I let the sentence trail away. They're both looking at me quizzically.

"The fact is," Goldie says at last, "you're not really making an effort to tell us anything. You're looking over our shoulders at the distant West, and trying to prove to them that they too can be mythologised."

Goja blinks with her one good eye. "Yes."

"All right then, I'll stop looking over my shoulder. I'll look at you—straight in the eye. *But I don't want you to disapprove of me!"*

They consider being embarrassed, then brush that aside. Goja says quite gently, "Hey, can't you forget we have that power? We've been dead for a while. We're equals now."

Goldie grins, "What are you afraid of telling us? That you're a lesbian? That you've had love affairs with women? I could tell you about lovers I've had, or haven't had."

"I could tell you about how my son was conceived," Goja puts in, "whether in love or in drunkenness, whether in passion or in dreariness."

"I could tell you about your grandfather."

Are they teasing me? I feel awkward and ashamed though I don't quite know why. Also confused. How stop their mouths? How discuss these things with elders?

"It's improper to tell me things about my grandfather if we are in the relationship of grandchild to grandmother," I say primly. "And if we are not, then perhaps it's irrelevant?" *Do the dead maintain a relationship with the living?*

Goja seems to have heard my thought. "If the living do," she answers. "Nobody wants to be unkind to you. To cut you off."

They've begun reading what's inside my mind. Well, that was what I wanted, wasn't it? *But I must speak to you as equals?*

"Yes."

It's a feat of the imagination I'm incapable of.

"That's because there's something you want."

What?

"Approval. Charity of sorts."

Well, why not?

"No, that's what we want."

And if I could give it?

"Then you could talk to us."

For a while Goja and Goldie sit in silence. We would like to talk.

You want me to understand that you are sexual creatures?

"Yes."

That you have suffered pain?

"Yes."

That you have been hurt and humiliated? Even violated?

"Yes."

That you are not particularly noble?

"Yes."

That you can be foolish and sad?

"Yes."

Why?

"Why not? You said you were interested in us."

And you want me to tell you about the West?

"Yes."

As though we were friends?

"Yes."

I don't know how to tell you. The West was a forest of words. The West was a language. But I will try. I will try to tell you about Paramour, what she was like.

11
PARAMOUR

Paramour's my friend. We walk about in the woods together. She is a wood nymph. She is the owner of the forest. I am her friend. I'm allowed to come and go as I please. It's a special privilege reserved for her friends. Paramour is not a grand dame. She's a woodland creature. She's other things too: an old woman, a precocious newcomer, perhaps a genius, certainly a goddess.

In the forest Paramour and I spend a great deal of our time talking:

Shall we strip leaves from trees, and offer
words like so many objects?
I would rather offer myself.

In this forest Paramour and I can luxuriate There will be—obviously—leaves to be eaten, and leaves with which we may sew ourselves a covering, leaves perhaps even for shelter, leaves for burning, leaves for mourning, leaves—ah, leaves that fail and fall, and turn colour, leaves that disappear. We could make an entire allegory of leaves and after the flurry of leaves subsides, we could lie down. Or we could look at each other in a leafless forest, shivering and naked.

I'm at home in this forest. The trees are friendly by definition. They are unfriendly only when I choose to be frightened. Paramour, of course, lives in this forest. She is the forest. Under enchantment anything is possible. Identity is lost, and with it fear. I'm a fawn in this forest. I put my head in her lap. The leaves and sunlight brush her nakedness—as I would, as I do. She feels my head against her thigh. She feels my tongue brush her hair. I embrace each tree trunk, each leafy branch to its very tip. For a while the forest and I float on darkness.

But the forest is not merely a place for pleasure. Sometimes I understand I'm trespassing here, or that at best I'm here on sufferance. Other people have laid claim to this forest. They say it belongs to their ancestors. They say they will not tolerate any unseemly behaviour, at least not from anyone other than themselves. In this forest women do not make love to women. In this forest men are centaurs. And the women? Are as secret and delicious as truffles. And the men are not centaurs? The men are pigs?

But that too is an enchantment, someone else's enchantment. In this forest, for all I know, there's a handsome knight whom a woman awaits with passionate lust. In this forest there are two handsome knights who wrestle each other in a celebration of muscle against muscle. In this forest there's a grunting and thumping, which, for all I know, gives satisfaction.

Words have to give desire shape, then clothe that shape, deck and bedeck it. Otherwise desire remains a lump. Desire itself must be made desirable. So that? The object of desire may be courted with the garments of desire, robed in splendour, or disrobed to reveal an even greater splendour. Is the glory of the Beloved just as illusory as the Emperor's robes?

There will come a time, my dear Paramour, when the forest no longer grows, when it is made of ceramics or metal. And as we stand under the trees, wittering on about our youth, the leaves will fall, each one so heavy and lethal, that it will be like a rain of boulders and we will be lucky if these leaves fail to kill us.

How does the forest cope with fear? And with reality? Surely even in an enchanted forest, one bangs one's head against a tree trunk? Meaning?

"Meaning," Goldfish Grandma and Goja interject, "that instead of daydreaming under the pretext that that is what you're supposed to do, why don't you say in plain English exactly what happened?"

English isn't plain. English is exotic, English is foreign. And anyway you don't understand it. I'm explaining it to you. In the form of Paramour—

"WHAT HAPPENED?"

What happened was this. She was Circe. She was Aphrodite. We made love. And then we didn't.

"What was she like?"

I saw roses damask'd red and white. Her voice was gentle, soft and low. She was exactly who she was supposed to be. Her speech and gestures had been written down. I desired her by definition.

"And that's the truth?" Both Goja and Goldie sound incredulous. Is that because they're Indian or because they're heterosexual?

"Neither!" Goldie says with some irritation, but she doesn't explain.

It's some of the truth, I tell them soberly.

"Without words you would not have loved her?"

Without words I would not have loved her quite so much.

I continue. Of course there are times when Paramour rejects me.

"My true troubadour, my manly minion, is a pink man," Paramour says, "not you, not you."

Since I'm a woman, a lesbian, and an Indian, I am an alien three times over. I hang my head. How can Paramour be so cruel? But it's a game. I know that. She knows that. It's a game she has played over and over. She is cruel, only—only because that's how it goes. She can't help herself.

Goldfish Grandma disrupts my account. "But what really happened?" She likes facts, Goldie does.

"And so do I," Goja interjects.

They're listening now. They really want to know. Did my paramour reject me? Yes, I tell them, over and over. Beasts. Why do they want to know? Isn't the tale of Paramour in the enchanted wood enough for them? *"But did you bleed?"* No. No blood. No real pain. Just unreal pain. When it hurts and hurts. When there is extraordinary pain, but no blood. Nothing to show for it, for all that hurt. *"Then what happened?"* Then we lived happily ever after.

"Don't patronise us!" Goja mutters.

"So Paramour is cruel?" Goldie muses. "See, you shouldn't have gone abroad. You should have stayed at home. India is for Indians. It's a much nicer place."

Goja glares at her, and, for once, Goldie notices and has the grace to look ashamed.

I wish Goja and Goldie wouldn't interrupt so much. I carry on.

But ought not Paramour to have a voice of her own, speak for herself, find her tongue? SHE IS PARAMOUR, a mythical monster, the Lady of a Thousand Million Tongues. Perhaps she is Fire—and we, all the poets there ever were, are her flames, tiny flames that shoot out of her, live and die, and contribute to her fire. A pleasing fancy. But does it please her?

She does, after all, have a voice of her own. She does not need the thousand million tongues of eager poets. She has a laugh of her own, a view of her own. She says: "I am a foreigner in my own country. I cannot see the wood for the trees. If the wood belongs to me, then the trees don't. If the trees belong to me, then the forest doesn't. Don't you understand? This is Canada. I am a native among foreign trees. And I look to you, the foreign one, the exotic one, the one who is an Indian and not a native, for company. Together we shall make a throng, well, at least, we'll make a twosome. In this country everyone is lonely."

That's what Paramour says. Well, that is what she says sometimes.

I ask her, "What is the difference between you and me?"

She replies that I have choices; but that for her there is only the snow, there is no other country.

I argue, "For everyone there's another country."

"Yes," she says, "there is another country. It isn't here. It's elsewhere. It's across the ocean. That is where the forest is—the one in which we met. Don't you understand? Even that forest is lost. It probably flourished in another century."

"Where is 'here'?" I ask Paramour.

"Here is elsewhere," she tells me, "and I am not Paramour. You are Paramour."

I smile slyly, but she's looking in the mirror and doesn't smile back. "Narcissus!" I call out.

"Echo!" she snaps back.

It's only a game. She says she's not Paramour; but when it suits her, she seizes the prerogative.

"This is cold Canada," she says emphatically. "And whoever and whatever you might be, I'm patriotic."

"Does that mean loving this forest, these trees, these leaves?" I ask, doing my best to look naive. I despair of looking innocent.

"Yes," she says, and "No," she says.

When I stare, she says that both answers are correct.

"Wot about being Injun?" I throw in.

"You mean East Indian, don't you?"

"No, *you* mean East Indian—wot about it?"

"What about it?"

"Can an Injun love this forest?"

She shrugs. "How should I know. It's not my business."

"Yes, it is."

"How? Why?"

"Because we're standing here talking to each other. Because we're contiguous. Because you're anglophone. Because we both inhabit the same forest, whichever forest you say it is."

Goja and Goldie peer over my shoulder and snigger at the text like a pair of schoolgirls.

"Didn't you do any work?" enquires Goja. I think she finds the romance of Paramour and her Lesbian Lover puzzling.

How can you ask that when in cold Canada I worked so hard and heroically? I, who had never so much as boiled an egg, did boil eggs, sweep floors, make beds . . . And I earned money—partly to live, and partly in order to buy you presents. I was doing my best to expiate guilt, undergo suffering. You see, once I found myself at the bottom of the heap, I understood clearly what you had suffered, what servants suffered. Don't you remember that on my first trip home I brought back presents for all the servants—well, many of them—which I had paid for with my own sweat and blood?

"No."

All that effort to be answered only with a monosyllable?

"Yes."

"Anyhow it's not very interesting," Goldie mutters. "We see you very clearly—blood, sweat, effort, suffering, etcetera—presumably in the name of Charity, but the trouble is—"

The trouble is I was never in love with Charity. I thought her worthy, but not glamorous.

Goja and Goldie nod sagely, "You were in love with yourself being in love with Charity. Nothing to do with Charity. You were very young."

But that's no excuse!

Goja and Goldie carry on kindly, "You've been in love with Paramour all these years."

She created the enchantment—

Now they're sniggering, "And you fell for it. Modish metaphors, timeworn truths—the whole kitch and caboodle!"

I don't think it's reasonable of Goldie and Goja to be quite so unkind. I suspect that underneath their banter they're really quite cross because I didn't love them better.

12
PAIN THE MEASURE?

"My dear," said Love laughing,
"I cannot compete
with God, Death
or your own Ego."

It's not true that the West is made up of ink and paper, or of images on screens. Something intractable and obdurate remains, however much it's dressed in words. People in the West were capable of being hurt, and were hurt. Is pain a measure of reality? They also felt pleasure. And they lived, and died. Like you, Goja, like you, Goldie, many and many went under the hill. But here you are now listening to me. Here you are being intelligent, attentive, even sympathetic, while I try to explain.

Paramour was a woman with two young children. She was not a goddess. She had left her husband and was bringing them up on her own. She tried to do her duty. She was a scholar and a dreamer. She wanted to live fully, but was often tired. And yes, she was enchanting—that too, but not to herself, only to me. To herself she was often weary. What was wanted was Charity. What was offered was Desire, which doesn't do much for anyone, except perhaps for the person who experiences it. It can be insistent at worst, tedious at best; and yet it's a god—Kama, Madan, Eros, Aphrodite. Paramour wanted me to be aware of her everyday life: the tuna sandwiches, the baby-sitting, the papers to be marked, the snowsuits into which her children had to be zipped. What I saw instead was high romance, extreme "cruelty" and extreme grief: a scenario worked out in my own mind for which the music of Wagner—had I known it—would have been barely adequate. What went on was a mixture of the lyrical and heroic, undercut by the self-consciously ironic—more like the modes in Northrop Frye than in the *Natya Shastra*, but then, Goldie, perhaps that's to be expected?

A row of peonies led to her front door. And because I entered that house with such breathlessness, the tight balls of the peonies about to burst open remain so forever, and the anticipation of being in her arms, however romantic—and therefore unreal?—still creates a murmur like the murmur of grass. How can I explain this to you? You were, I presume, heterosexual? And in your universe perhaps it's unimaginable that a woman should feel such desire for a woman? Perhaps it's unimaginable that a woman should feel desire at all? Or imaginable only in stories and myths, but not in real life? Desire cannot have anything to do with one's own granddaughter—that would cause a scandal—and certainly not with one's own grandmother or an elderly servant—that would not be seemly. Does that make you smile? There are more things . . . ?

It's assumed that the aged, particularly aged women, do not feel anything other than a benign maternal love. They shed their blessings and feel no desire. I call you "aged", but how old were you really? Goja, you were ageless, because that is convenient in a servant. And Goldfish Grandma—no disrespect is meant—

though you were forty-two when I was born, and eighty-four when you died, in my eyes you never aged at all. But then, for me, you were never young. I suppose that too was convenient. Does respect demand we keep our distance? Let's break that taboo, so that, at last, we might acknowledge each other. All three of us were children once. Already death has overtaken you, and one day I shall die.

You point out that acknowledging each other is all very well, but that I'm doing the talking and you're doing the listening. What can I say? I'm willing to write down whatever you've told me, but you didn't tell me much.

You didn't ask.

It would not have been seemly.

You should have tried. Explaining the West is quite unnecessary. They've been explaining themselves to themselves and to everyone else for several centuries. They are quite convinced of their own humanity; what needs explaining is ours to them. We know a great deal about them, but as you found out, they don't know much about us. From their point of view it isn't necessary. You've said yourself that servants know a great deal about their masters—they have to know. Don't you find it significant that all three of us understand English?

What? Even Goja?

More than you think.

Yes, all right. I concede your point. I do what I can. I've lived in the West and in the East. Perhaps I'm trying to understand what the Emperor looks like when the Emperor is displayed to foreign eyes. No, all I'm doing is telling you a winter's tale, while time passes, has passed, is passing. I don't want to tell you all about the West. I just want to tell you what it was like for me. We are, all of us, both foolish and worthwhile—and extremely temporary. You say you'll listen? Ah, my captives.

So you see, there was a row of peonies and, in the back garden, a peach tree. Once when I plucked the peaches for her, they were like golden planets hung about my head. She gave me paradise. Gave me? It discomfited her. She wanted me to see her as she really was. Perhaps she wanted me to see her as she saw herself. What? Displace my myth for hers? And then perhaps to love her, to love the image of herself that she loved, or did not love, but perceived as accurate. Is that what people want? Not to be adored or worshipped, but merely to be loved because they exist.

There's a story about you, Goldie. My grandfather was given two photographs, one of you and one of your sister, to choose between. It's said that he stuck a flower on each of the photographs. I can see that so clearly. It must have been a *parijatak* flower. He crushed the small orange stem and the white petals. Its own crushed life must have made the flower stick in place. For a while afterwards his fingers must have smelled of the perfume. It's said her flower fell. Yours stayed in place, and so he chose you.

I find it hard to believe that he could have chosen anyone other than you. But how did this story make *you* feel? Did you feel fortunate because you had married a Raja? And because your image had been preferred? But how did it make you feel that you became a queen all by virtue of the stickiness of a flower? And how did he feel? By what good fortune was he adopted by the Raja, his uncle? By what good fortune are any of us born? In the West they had a writer called Butler—nobody reads him much nowadays, but then nobody reads much anyway—who pointed out that in the wide world to be fortunate is to be meritorious and that's how it goes. You are deserving because you were fortunate. You are fortunate because you were deserving. Karma? Great stuff for the status quo wallahs.

I was saying that Paramour wanted to be loved for who she really was. It makes sense. It's what we all want. It's a necessity or perhaps a cure. A cure for what? Why do I need a cure? For the injuries done me as I grew up. You start back. Am I about to accuse you? Why not? You see, that too is different between the East and the West, between your half century and mine. In the Country of the Kind—I mean yours and mine—everyone takes their chances, and if many are maimed, well, that's how it is. Everyone shuts up. But here in the West—well in some parts of the West, some of the time—they believe in psychobabble, they believe in pity, kindness, compassion. They believe that if somebody starts whining, somebody else is supposed to put an arm around their shoulders and offer comfort. They believe that to scream and shout, "I hurt" is somehow better than screaming and shouting, "I hate."

Goja? Goldie? I don't want to concede that in this respect people in the West are better than we are; but they might be. They are perhaps a little obsessed with suffering, but at least they attend to it; whereas for us suffering is just an ordinary fact and we walk by it as though it didn't matter or didn't exist.

But you say you want to know about Paramour, not about suffering. (They're connected, you know.) You want to be told what happened to her. Was she real? How did it end? Paramour the goddess goes on forever—well, at least she goes on as long as the forest lasts. She still enchants, remains beautiful. But the other woman, the one who lived in the house with peonies, who made tuna sandwiches, who brought up two children, she is mortal. Over the years her children grew up, the weather marked her, she broke an ankle, she wrote a book, she had other lovers, she painted pictures.

From time to time we write to each other. She too remembers the taste of snow. Does it mean anything if we remember the same thing? And what does it mean if for me sometimes the snow was ecstatic? The wind was ecstatic. The evergreen trees. The cross-country skiing. If for me cold Canada was sometimes ecstatic and all because I loved her, then what was unreal? The ecstasy was real, but the love was less so. Some of it was a cold, crying, chilling need at times made glamorous and gorgeously robed.

And so for some years Paramour and I loved and fought, loved and fought: ecstasy punctuated by the need to earn a living, the need to work and the need to practise the art of poetry. That life is gone. It's the same for you I suppose. Does the practice of poetry make you laugh? Does it seem like the occupation of a dilettante, particularly in comparison to bringing up children? Or being a servant and being forced to bring up other people's children? Does it anger you, Goldie, that you were not allowed to earn a living? Use your brains? That the two of you had no choice? That I made choices? And that you somehow had to find a virtue, something worthwhile, in necessity? Or perhaps you feel contempt for me because I made the wrong choices? Because I suffered unnecessary hardships?

Suddenly such comparisons generate fellow feeling. You are not my elders and my betters. You are like me: vivid for a while, muddled, struggling, and even while alive, dying slowly.

13
I TOO AM NOBLE

"I am lying in the mud,"
I groaned at Charity,
"and am so humiliated,
I might even
have achieved humility."
Charity disagreed.
"Well, then what's required?"
"Not sure.
You could try standing up and suffering
less noisily."
I rose from the mud.
How long can one stay there?
"My suffering matters."
I was adamant.
And Charity thoughtfully, "Yes, that's it.
If you thought it didn't, then perhaps
you'd achieve humility."

When I tried to tell you about the West or the West about you I never quite got the response I wanted. Once I told you about an old man who used to yell at me as I walked down the street. It had made me feel angry and vulnerable, but you just laughed. I thought it was because you as the Ranisaheb had never been humiliated; now I suspect I was wrong. But shouldn't you take some responsibility for the fact that your grandeur couldn't protect me at all? To which you reply—with feigned surprise—that you thought I was against grandeur and that I was trying to deconstruct the glamour attached to privilege. You then add that no one had wanted me to stay in the West. The family had always said: "Why be a third-class citizen and go to live somewhere where you're not even wanted?" And lastly you point out that your own power had diminished considerably—you had no power and were unable to protect anyone.

Yes, okay, but let me describe something to you. A September day, Toronto, in the seventies. I'm standing at the bus stop waiting for the university bus to take me to the college where I work. A red-headed young man comes up to me. He wants to know whether I've encountered much racism here—you know, people looking down on me and all that. He himself is a liberal, he assures me. He would like to help those who are less fortunate than himself. I feel patronised and would like to say something cutting in return, but can't think of anything. I haven't understood yet that being despised doesn't make me despicable. And like a fool I deny I've encountered racism or anything like that.

Well, Goldie? Is your granddaughter not all that grand?

This kind of thing happened again and again. People in an academic environment are particularly subject to a lukewarm liberalism, which allows them to indulge in *noblesse oblige* whenever they feel so inclined. It's hardly surprising then that anything I had to say about my family background was not palatable. They preferred to believe I had come to the West to improve myself. One day a colleague asked me in the Faculty Lounge whether my family in India had a bathroom. It was particularly astonishing that she asked since her parents were British and had lived in India. She had meant to insult me and I was duly insulted. But Goja? Goldie? There are people in India who don't have a bathroom. Was I insulted because of being compared with them? And therefore did I concur with her notion that that was somehow despicable? *It is this that angers me so much: the way we bash up people and then spit on them for being bashed!*

Through the seventies in the West the breastbeating white liberal types were common in the universities. They would approach someone they identified as in some way socially inferior and then apologise profusely to them. They would moan that they couldn't help being white or male or hetero-sexual or something or the other that identified them as one of the privileged. It was so clear that their *mea culpa* was dishonest. It was the identification, I think, the smirk on their faces as they confessed—to their shame!—that they were, in fact, "noble", in their own way privileged! It would have been funny, had it not been so frequent and so very tedious.

Ah, but well then, Goldie, as your granddaughter, am I not, at least a little noble? And well, then Goja were you not, in fact, our servant? It's like a slap in the face. Our? Servant? To have to say this is so deeply shaming. Who shall we castigate for these words? The English language? Because it makes churls of the poor, and happily ennobles the rich and powerful? If I had stayed at home? Is Marathi less racist, less sexist, less class—and caste—conscious?

The family said and still says, "Why go abroad and be a third-class citizen?" Goja, what do you say? If I had stayed at home, could you and I have been truly family? If I'm a third-class citizen, does *that* make me a third-rate human being? Or if I am a first-class citizen, does that make me a third-rate human being? I should like to point out to all the queens and princesses that ever there were that no woman is a first-class human being. She's second class. And anyway I was a lesbian, so presumably I would have been a third-class human being in any society, wherever it was in the wide world.

Let's see.

To deprive human beings of their self-respect is a cruel thing. This is what's done to lesbians and gays.

To exploit human beings and then to despise them for being exploited is worse. This is done to the poor, also to servants.

But what is fiendish is to exploit human beings and then to persuade them that in that very exploitation lies their self-respect, their place in society, indeed, their duty. And that's what they do to women and to servants. That's what they do when they set up a stable hierarchy, and then Goldie, and then Goja, the glory of the masters is the glory of the servants.

This last we three should understand well. We lived through the end of it. But hey, you two, what's getting established is neo-feudalism. Under the new system I'm a serf of capitalism. And I hate it. Would I prefer to be a lord? Yes. And therein I'm corrupt.

"That's all very well," Goja interrupts, "but I saw no disgrace in being your servant."

There was no disgrace, I reply. The disgrace lay in being your masters. I can see that Goldie doesn't agree, but for the time being she has decided to be tolerant. I carry on.

I hadn't understood how power operates or at least I hadn't worked it out until I got involved with feminism and gay liberation. Christine helped me.

Who is Christine? Another Paramour?

Yes. No. For several years she was my friend and partner. She's still my friend. Goja, you never met her because by then it was too late. But Goldie you could have met her.

Well, why didn't you bring her along on one of your trips home and introduce her?

Too honest.

What?

She was too honest to lie about herself or her relation to me, and then you'd have refused to see her.

You have to be sensible you know. In India these things cause a scandal. A little discretion would have made a world of difference.

Goldie, it's precisely this "discretion" that has done so much damage! You and your lot go on and on about the warrior caste, about the values of honour and courage and all that stuff. Do you think it required no courage to come out and say explicitly as so many people did: "Yes, I'm lesbian, or yes, I'm homosexual," and so gradually remove the disgrace from those words?

That was in the West. As long as it didn't reach India, it doesn't matter.

Goldie! The publishers sold my books. The newspapers published reviews!

Well, all I can say is I'm glad I didn't live to see it. It wasn't necessary to make all this fuss. Just creates a scandal.

And you say you loved me? Can't you understand? The real scandal in India is the huge discrepancy between the rich and the poor!

Stop raising your voice. It's disrespectful. And in any case poverty in India is a vast problem. It is so vast no one can do anything. I did some social work. What else could I have done? At least I stayed in India. You ran away.

What choice did I have?

I feel bitter and angry. I turn to Goja and ask what she thinks.

But Goja turns away. She says clearly and distinctly: *What difference does it make what either of you thinks is the true scandal?*

14
THE CROSS-EXAMINATION

Goldie and I aren't speaking to each other. Goja is silent. I'm left alone. Perhaps I'm better off without the two of them. When we try to talk we just cause each other pain.

Is there no reality in which the three of us could have lived happily together, without pain, fuss or mutual recrimination? Where we could have just let the others be themselves and loved them for who they were?

It would be nice to live in a peopled forest, a place where the trees call out to me, speak my name (and pronounce it properly). I could live happily there with Goja and Goldie, be whoever I was supposed to be . . . Well, perhaps not. I went away.

Goja, you and Goldie stayed where you were. Were you allowed to be who they said you were supposed to be? Dreadful irony. You had to be who you were supposed to be! But in the Forest of Heart's Desire might we have lived happily together? You by the Indian Ganges side could salvation find—your heart's desire which the family never gratified. All you wanted was to go to Kashi, and to bathe in the Ganges, such a small thing—why wasn't it arranged? I by the tide of Humber—a river I've actually seen—would gather hazel nuts, which, I think, you would like. Then you, Goldie and I would sit around a fire and roast corn. We'd put butter on the corn, even clarified butter—*toop*, salt and red pepper and a bit of lemon juice. Yes, I know, where would we get all these things? In a forest who would light the fire, and what about Goldie's teeth, and your teeth, and now mine? And how would we make space and time concur? How bend them so that we might meet?

Goja and Goldie shrug: "You are the controller of this forest. You are the controller of language. You can say anything, do anything. Whatever you say has to be. Our function is to listen. Listen up. Listen here. Listen to what you say. In short, do what you want us to do. Say what you want us to say. Be who you want us to be."

Goja! Goldie! It's not like that. To be the sole controller of language is to be no one, nobody. The words fall away, the leaves drop off and one stands there shivering. Language requires a Speaker and a Listener. Then something more. The Speaker and the Listener must exchange roles, take each other's places, and understand somehow what it's like. You are not my audience, you're my auditors. And I have to present my true account. Don't you see?

At last you smile. At heart you're kindly, and you don't point out that you're doing me a favour by listening. But you do smile. Is listening an act of charity?

Perhaps you say, "The sound of one hand clapping, one wing flapping, is insufficient. We will lend you our strength."

Goja! I didn't want to batter your ears. I wanted to record the texture of your clothes, the feel of the sun, the haze of dust, the taste of air, the smell of that time. Goldie! I loved you both. Against time I can only fling words, which disintegrate like snowballs, or flop like flowers. And yet just flinging them achieves something; it generates a flicker that could ignite consciousness. Then we remember, then we dream and each living thing that ever was flares into life. I misunderstood the poets. I thought they were bragging about the power to confer immortality. The power of poetry isn't that at all. It is only the power to say that every living thing flamed and died; and that it did so matters.

Even the poets have served you, Charity, though in ignorance sometimes and in despite!

Goja and Goldie clap, but it's half-hearted. I have to accept them as they are. At last I say, slowly, painfully, "Don't you understand? *I miss you, but you exiled me!*"

Goldie isn't having that. "No! You exiled yourself. You have to take responsibility for what you did."

This time I turn away. We sit in silence. Isolated. We're asking ourselves whether we would really want each other back.

After a while Goja speaks. "What will you do now? Leave us?"

They know very well I can't leave them. "What about you, will you leave me?"

"We can't leave you," Goldie says gently. "We're interlinked."

"And Charity?"

"What about her?"

"She's missing."

If only she would come, it would be all right; but Goja and Goldie are wearing that disillusioned look the old sometimes wear. We wait in the clearing. In the space between us perhaps she will appear. Surely we love one another? In spite of everything we love one another! But if she really were to appear, what would we say?

Perhaps Goja would say: "Charity, how could you allow me to be so poor? To have my life so used and abused?"

Goldie would say: "Charity how could you allow me to be so

thoughtless? To fritter away my life doing a little bit of harm and very little good?"

And I would say: "Charity, how could you allow me to be so self-indulgent?"

I know what Charity would say to Goldie and to me; but what would she say to Goja? I think Goja and Charity should have a battle till Charity shed tears of blood. (That is very Christian. Or perhaps it's a heresy? After all, in this version for whose sins is Charity weeping?) Perhaps we should all weep, but I don't know what good weeping does. Washes away the grit. Improves eyesight.

"Goja! Goldie! I've just realised. Whether we laugh or cry we are three old women, because by now I too am old. It's not each other we should be questioning. We should all be asking *her* questions."

And then suddenly, as large as life, in the middle of the clearing, she does appear. She doesn't look like Saraswati or Parvati or any other goddess really, though, I suppose, she could be any of them. She looks like Goja or Goldie or me or anyone. But the worst of it is she doesn't look mournful. She's smiling and laughing. Is she laughing at us? It's too much to bear. I get to my feet, and with the two of them watching, I plead for some answers.

"Charity, what would you have us do? Should we summon our loves, all our loves? Dead grandmothers? Dead servants? Dying granddaughters? Should we summon them all and take our leave of them? Is that love?"

"If they vanish anyway and we have no choice, then can that be love?"

"Is acceptance love?"

"How can the acceptance of death be love?"

"How can there be love where there is death?"

At which point Charity says: How can there be love if there is no death? The immortals probably don't need any love.

"Are you mortal, Charity?"

I am mortal.

"Like us?"

Like you.

"But we are unable to love. How can you be yourself if you are like us?"

You are able to love.

"But we don't know how. The love overbalances and we all fall down."

Yes.

"So don't you see what we're saying? We are not like you. We fail. We fail often."

It doesn't matter.

"It does matter!"

There you are then.

"But what is the right answer? Should we care or not care?"

Both.

"Should we try or not try?"

"Does it matter or not matter?"

"Should we grieve or not grieve?"

"Should we strip away hope?"

"Should we be hopeful?"

"Should we strip away fear?"

"Should we be fearful?"

"Should we have no faith? Only clear sight?"

"Should we keep our faith though we live in the thickest darkness?"

"Should we live?"

Yes!

"Should we die?"

Since you must.

"But Charity how can there be love in a world filled with death?"

I have already answered.

"Charity! What matters?"

"Does winning matter?"

No.

"Does losing matter?"

No.

"Does death matter?"

Yes.

"Does death matter?"

No.

"Charity which is the right answer?"

Rightly understood, both are right answers.

"Charity will I die?"

Yes.

"Is that fair?"

Fair?

"Yes, is it fair?"

No.

"Then why must I die?"

I don't know.

"Then what can you do? What can you know?"

I can only love.

"And I?"

Yes, you too.

"But it hurts."

Yes.

"Is that fair?"

I don't know.

"What can you know? What can you do?"

I can only love.
"Charity, am I like you?"
Yes.
"Charity, am I unlike you?"
Yes.
"It's hard to be like you."
Yes.
"It's easy sometimes!"
Yes.
"What is the right answer?"
You know what it is.

PART III

LATER

15

BULLET-PROOF BODIES

Love said, "Be patient. In due course—"
"The acorn will turn into an oak tree?
And the oak—oh, wait for it!—will turn
into a ship's mast, blonde floorboards,
a vast dining table, anything!"
Love smiled, "And in due course
you will grow as tall as the oak,
your shadow lengthening—" *"Yes," I cried,*
"beyond evening and into the night!"
"And in due course you will acquire—"
"A monumental patience? But I won't be smiling!
I'll be laughing at grief!"
                                        Love flinched;
and for the time being that satisfied me.
But later I heard my own voice,
"Love is not a longing. Patience
is needful. Be dispassionate. Love is."

Watery sunlight filters through the leaves of tall oaks. Goja and Goldie look about them. It's obvious that from time to time someone clears the ground between the trees.

"Why have you brought us here?" Goldie asks.

"To show you where I live," I tell them. "This is England. Here the language clings to the landscape—subject to time and change of course. These are English oaks." Goja and Goldie nod, but seem unimpressed. We're inside the "D" of an iron-age fort. At the far end of the clearing two people are walking their dogs. They are polite English and leave us alone.

"Why did you move to England?"

"I fell in love."

They both sigh. I know what they're thinking. "Another Paramour?"

"Yes, but this time with nothing at cross purposes. We both knew we'd have to find something tougher and more lasting than just romantic love. We've lived together now for many years."

"Why did you move to England? Was she English?"

"No, Gill is Australian, but she lived in England. She had a child. It was easier for me to move."

Goja wants to know whether there's much difference between the Canadians, the English and the Australians.

I tell her that from their point of view there's a great deal of difference, from our point of view not much.

"I know about the English, the British—what is the difference? They came to India and ruled over us," Goja says.

Goldie nods. She knows about the British as well. She had to deal with them. Many years ago there was a flurry in the household and for once Goldie had no time for me—all because the Governor was coming to dinner.

"Are you happy in England?" Goldie asks. "Are they nice to you there?"

I shrug. "They're neither nice, nor nasty. They know more about India than the Canadians did, but the India they are in love with is *their* India. They use us as a backdrop on which they were once able to strut. I don't like it, but I suppose it's understandable."

"Are you happy at last?" Goldie goes on. "This Gill, who I never met, is she good to you?"

"We try hard to be good to each other. We have our failings. Gill has been to India several times. We've been discreet, but I do not think they really want us. I wanted her to see where I grew up, what it was like."

After a pause I add, "It was a grief to me that she never met you." But I find myself thinking, what good would it have done?

Goja and Goldie are staring at me anxiously. I realise that they don't want me to be hurt. I also realise that for them I'll always be five years old. I burst out at them, "I'm nearly the same age as you now! How can I always be the child, the Little One? I cannot! I am not! And yet, the way you look at me! I understand why as a child I was able to voyage so freely between you. I needed love and would have asked the Ranisaheb or the servant. I'd have asked a cat, a dog, a tree trunk. You gave me love when I needed it most. And for that I honour and respect you—"

"But?"

Goldie is waiting. This is my chance to say whatever I think needs to be said, but I'm not sure what I want to say. I take a deep breath.

"But I think an apology is in order."

"Really?" Goldie's voice is icy. The *grande dame* is well to the fore. "Who do you think should apologise to whom and for what?"

I'm in for it now. "I think you should apologise to me. And I think you should apologise to Goja."

But Goja snaps, "If you want an apology, you ask for one. I'll speak for myself."

And Goldie is incredulous. "You want *me* to apologise to *you*?"

"Yes."

"For what?" She really doesn't know.

"For sending me away. For not letting me live honourably and peacefully in my own country and in my own home."

"You went away! And you can return."

"On your terms! 'Live quietly and silently. Come by yourself. Don't rock the boat. Don't cause a scandal. Do what we say.' It's inhuman!"

Goldie really is angry now. "You disgraced yourself! You disgraced the family! The best thing you did was to stay away!"

That hurt. I'm frightened and can hardly breathe. I look to Goja for help, but she's staying out of this. At last I say, "I did nothing shameful. A society that punishes people for no good reason—that is shameful."

Goldie replies with some disdain. "We are talking about India, not the West. Here people do not do whatever they wish and misbehave, especially not women."

I make one last appeal. "I did not do exactly what I liked or misbehave. Goldie, I've told you how it was. Why can't you understand? Why won't you relent?"

Goldie says a little less harshly, "In India things are different. If only you had been willing to be a little discreet . . ."

"To be 'discreet' is to admit that there's reason to be ashamed!"

Goldie and I look at each other. Then she says clearly and distinctly, "Let's get this clear. You think that *I* owe *you* an apology?"

"Yes."

"Don't be ridiculous! You are to blame!"

I had forgotten what Marathas can be like. In that peaceful clearing the leaves overhead seem to absorb what's being said. More grief, more pain—in any landscape. I don't want to continue. I'm afraid of Goldie's anger. I think it could destroy me, but I do continue.

"I'm not ridiculous. You're intelligent enough to know that sexuality in itself is not a moral issue. It's the willingness to use it to hurt other people that is really immoral."

But Goldie loses patience. "I am not interested in your Western liberalism. And anyway as a woman you had more freedom than I ever had. I don't understand why you weren't content. Even if I had wanted to, I couldn't have changed an entire society. Being the Ranisaheb did not make me invulnerable, invincible or even immortal." She pauses and then enunciates each word. "I grew old. I was ill and now I'm dead."

This is brutal. Why is Goldie so impatient with me? Doesn't she know how much her death hurt? Doesn't Goja realise how much I cared? I still care. I remember how Goldie slipped and fell. I wasn't there. I remember how she was put to bed and then didn't rise from that bed. I remember that I wasn't summoned. I remember she went into a coma. They told me she had bed sores. Because of her weight they couldn't move her. She had a grand funeral. For her funeral pyre they cut down sandalwood trees. But I wasn't there.

"Look," Goja tries to calm us down now, "whatever happened happened a long time ago. Don't you understand. You are alive. We are dead. We are helpless."

"But nothing has changed!"

"Then who are you really talking to? Who are you shouting at?"

At myself? At the pain? At the whole of India?

I don't answer her. Instead I ask, "Goja, what's the difference between the living and the dead?"

For a moment I think they're about to scold me for a lack of decorum, but having gone this far, what can I lose? I carry on. I decide to ask them something very specific.

"What's the difference between how you read the paper and how I read it?"

"Can't read," says Goja.

"I don't read," says Goldie. "Cataracts and eye strain."

They're being flippant and have relaxed a little, but they're still on their guard. Perhaps they think I'm going to force them to talk about mutual forgiveness. Well, perhaps I am.

"It's very simple," Goldie says suddenly. "If the paper announced that the war had come to the little English village where you live now, you would have to dodge the bullets, but we wouldn't. That's what it is."

Goja nods vigorously. I frown. They're having a game with me. Pain, I think suddenly. Bullet-proof bodies and a lack of pain—that defines the dead.

"Do you feel pain?" I ask them suddenly.

They look embarrassed.

"You look embarrassed!" I accuse them. "What does that mean? That once you're dead, nothing matters anymore? That what happens to the living is no longer your business?" Why am I so angry? Do I suspect that if they can no longer feel pain, they can no longer love? I think I'm angry because they can hurt me, but I cannot hurt them.

Goldie and Goja frown. They seem annoyed. "It's your imagination," Goldie mutters. "Anyway, I thought you were concerned with what had happened to us—with the past, not the present."

"It's all connected," I retort. "Besides, I think you ought to ask Goja's forgiveness."

As soon as I say this Goldie turns into a pillar of silence, but Goja blazes. The iridescent blues and greens in her *choli* burn. I realise I've stepped on Maratha pride, and have triggered that old reaction from the warriors' creed: "Klingons never apologise." And perhaps they never accept apologies? Perhaps they're right. Perhaps just saying "Sorry" would be a joke. The last time I was in India I heard someone say that Westerners are people who say "Sorry" all the time—and then push through. To say to Goja, "Bad luck, bad *karma*, very sorry, very sorry," would be worse than idiotic, it would be—

"Stupid! You stupid, talkative child!" I've never seen Goja so angry. I've offended her and would apologise, but she doesn't give me a chance. "You think you know something, but you know nothing!"

They stand beside each other: a column of silence and a column of fire. I'm cowed. They're older than me, wiser than me, bigger than me, probably even better than me. But there's something in what I'm saying, and it matters. "It matters," I mumble stubbornly.

"WHAT MATTERS?"

Now they're both shouting. Why are they shouting? In the past they didn't shout; but then in the past, I didn't ask too many questions. And anyway, servants couldn't shout, and Goldie was too grand to shout. Once when Goja was on her hands and knees, cleaning the floors, I said to her, "Don't wipe the floors." I didn't say, "I'll wipe them for you." But she said that Ranisaheb would want the floors cleaned. Clean floors are a wonderful thing. Why not? We all want clean floors, but who is supposed to clean them? I remember those stone floors, Shahabad stone and patterned tiles, in the house that has crumbled. Does the fact of servants make it an evil house even though I have good memories, and a few bad ones?

"What do you expect us to say?" Goldie asks. "Do you want to say to Goja that you regret the past? That you repent of it?

The past is the past, after all."

"What has been should not have been. Someone has to say it." I say it badly.

Goldie turns reasonable. That is when she's most dangerous. I've seen her slip a verbal noose around someone's neck and hang them casually in the course of a conversation. Now she asks nicely, "Do you want to ask Goja for her forgiveness?"

I'm suspicious, but I say, "Yes." What else can I say? I open my mouth. "Goja, will you—"

And Goja rages, "I don't want to be asked for my forgiveness!"

I shut my mouth. I can't very well say to Goja, "You have to pardon me. Please? Please!" The relatively rich turned mendicant? Another cheap trick! Not pleasing, and dangerous. Either put up or shut up. Give all you have unto the poor, or don't give it. But whatever you do, don't bleat. It isn't seemly. But bleating is a regular pastime for those of us who are neither loving, nor unkind.

I wish I was five years old again and could say, "Goja, tell me a story?" And perhaps she would.

I look down at the grass and twist a grass blade between my fingers. Eventually Goldie shakes her head. "We treat you like a five-year-old when you behave like one!"

And Goja says not unkindly, "What you really want is a happy ending."

"Yes," I agree. "Is that so unusual?"

16
REVOLUTIONARY ACTS

We're back on a hill in western Maharashtra. They say that where I live is pleasant enough—it's an "area of outstanding natural beauty"—but they find the relentless green surreal.

"Once upon a time," Goja begins, "there was a kingdom. It had people in it. There was a king and a queen, there were royal children, royal grandchildren—that's where you come in. You see, Little One, it's not that simple. There isn't just the Ranisaheb and you and me talking in the dark, chatting in private, meeting on a mountaintop and trying to make friends after two of us are dead. There was an entire society rooted in the past, rushing into the future and with sideways connections going this way and that. Not so easy to alter. To unwish one thing would have changed everything."

"I'm not sure about that," I interrupt.

And Goldie murmurs, "Yes, it would have changed the fabric of space and time. I think—"

"Will you be quiet!" Goja's voice overrides everyone.

There's a shocked silence. Goja has told the Ranisaheb to be quiet. Wow! It's a revolutionary act. A bit of me is gleeful. Also horrified. Servants don't talk to their—masters?—no, not masters, paymasters?—no—. People don't talk to my grandparents like that. I remember the old days. When we drove through the town, people would stop and bow down properly, glad to be recognised. The men in their white *kurtas* and *dhotis* —well, almost white—would do a *mujra*, the women would bend and do a *namaskar*. This was from a distance. When they got closer to my grandparents, when they could get close enough, they would—What is the matter with me! I sound like the British yearning for their Raj. It won't do. What has been, must not be. But Goja has insulted the Ranisaheb. Now what will happen?

"Nothing will happen," Goja informs me. She can read my mind? Well, why not. She's inside my head. Being alive, I have to carry them both. She adds, "I may have told the Ranisaheb to shut up, but I've done it when it no longer matters."

I realise that I too have waited till it no longer matters. All right, I'm a coward.

Goja glowers, and clears her throat. "The king of this kingdom wasn't fit to be king."

I'm amazed by Goja! But I can't let that go. "Why not?" I protest. "He cared about his people."

"A king," Goja declares sternly, "has to be much better than ordinary people. We look up to him, bow down to him, because he is King, because he is better than the rest of us."

We look up to someone, bow down to someone because they are powerful. But can I say that? Surely my grandfather was genuinely respected? What sort of game is Goja playing? Goldie and I glance at each other. Talking about who deserves to be king, deserves to be queen, deserves to be rich, deserves to be poor, could get very tricky.

"Exactly," says Goja, reading my mind effortlessly. "Now do be quiet and let me go on."

"But he *was* respected?" I plead with Goja. "And so was the Ranisaheb!" I glance at Goldie, who just looks grim.

"Sure he was respected," Goja replies, "as long as he had power. As he lost power he lost respect."

That's true enough. I remember the worn Persian carpet, the unpainted walls, the shortage of money and the general shabbiness of the last days. And I remember also that the people who had once sought him out learnt to ignore him. They pretended to be busy or engaged in something else or they looked another way. It makes me angry when I think of it. But isn't that exactly what I wanted—a more just and egalitarian society?

Time shall demolish the most evil emperor and the kindest king. But then that isn't the point.

I remember Tukaram, Goldie's chauffeur and my friend. Can a servant be a friend? When I spouted some of my democratic stuff, he said, "Well, persuade them then to give me a plot of land." I didn't persuade anyone to do anything. I'm not even sure I tried. He didn't pursue the matter. He had that resigned look in his eyes. I don't think he expected anything to happen, and nothing did happen, until one day he died of cancer.

This last time I was in India a new chauffeur—he worked for a cousin—was less than respectful to me. I put him in his place. But what is a chauffeur's place? Perhaps he was less than respectful because I was a woman or because I no longer lived in India. But did I do the right thing or the wrong thing? And would I have dared had something similar happened in Canada or in England? I know I should be ashamed, but a part of me feels that what I did was exactly right. I glance at Goja, but don't risk asking her what she thinks.

"There has to be some sort of social structure," I venture. "Are you proposing no king at all? Or perhaps someone else as king? Or . . ." I remember suddenly that the Indian princes had limited powers. In return for kowtowing to the British emperor, all they really had were their privy purses, and their titles, and a certain amount of being kowtowed to themselves . . . I wonder what Goldie makes of it.

"I agree with Goja," Goldie says suddenly. "The wrong people get made kings, ministers, prime ministers. I would have made a much better king. I had the brains, you see, and would have liked to have ruled."

I gape at her. Goldie a feminist?

She shakes her head impatiently. "No, no, I'm not a feminist or a communist." (Just an egoist! I think, but don't say it.) "Some people are more competent than others—that's all there is to it."

Goja fixes her with her one good eye and says confidently, "I'd have made a far better king than either you or him."

"You!" Goldie's incredulity is offensive. She finds the notion of Goja being her equal or even her superior completely unacceptable. It's very like my reaction to the chauffeur's behaviour.

But Goja isn't cowed. "I know how poor people live. I know what they need and want. I know what it's like to have almost nothing and still survive. You wouldn't have survived even for a week if you had had to live my life!"

I've thought this myself. It's not just that the ground is too hard to sleep on, or the food too coarse, the clothes too dirty, the physical labour too prolonged and too difficult. It's the germs. The germs would attack us and kill us with diseases. But I stick to my policy of saying nothing.

"It's not a matter of *being* one of the poor," Goldie says scornfully. "It's all a matter of *governing* the poor."

"If you were the King, what would you do for the poor?" Goja challenges. "What would be the point of having you as King?"

"I would," replies Goldie, "protect the poor."

"You and who else?"

"Me and my henchmen."

"And who would you protect them from?"

"From other feudals and their henchmen! It's the feudal system! Don't you understand anything? And you want to be King! It's not in your blood. It is in mine."

"How do you know it's not in mine? It could easily be in mine," protests Goja. "And what would you get out of being so noble and protecting everyone?"

"Tribute. The poor would serve and protect me and pay me taxes as well."

"But then *they* would be protecting *you*!"

"Yes. That's the beauty of it!" Goldie says impatiently. "They've got to be organised!"

My own grandmother expounding the protection racket! She sounds like a *mafiosa*, well, at least a fascist.

"I'm not any of those things," Goldie interrupts my thoughts indignantly. "I am an aristocrat."

"I could be just as good an aristocrat as you," Goja says scornfully. "In fact, better."

"How?"

"By caring about the poor."

"Huh! I would care about the poor," Goldie replies. "In my reign the poor would be happy—"

"To be poor?" Goja mocks her. "The servants would be happy to be servants? The women would be happy to be women? The rich would be happy to be rich?"

Goldie nods. "That's precisely what I do mean."

"What about lesbians?" I ask. "Would lesbians be happy to be lesbians?"

"No," Goldie replies crossly. "Lesbians would be happy *not* to be lesbians. Good government requires the exercise of some sort of control over people's lives!"

Well! If Goldie's going to be like that, I'll vote for Goja as King. "Goja! If you were King, you'd be nice to me, wouldn't you?"

She pats my head. "Of course, Little One. Why not? I was nice to you even when I wasn't a king."

Goldie too pats my head. "And I was nice to you even when I was a queen."

Is that all it amounts to—just a matter of who is nice to whom? Is that the point of Goja's tale?

I turn to her. "Please Goja," I ask, "why were you nice to me when you were only a servant?"

Perhaps now we can dispense with this talk of kings and queens and get at something truthful and real.

Goja says evenly, "It was my job."

That hurts. I don't say anything. After all, I too have some Maratha pride.

Then she relents. "How can I know whether or not I loved you when looking after you was compulsory—something I had to do, or else lose my job and suffer the consequences?"

What can I say? I shouldn't have asked. But I'm beginning to understand the point of Goja's tale: as long as Charity is confined to the private sphere, and Power to the public and political one—nothing works!

After a while Goja asks, "Did you love me?"

I don't know what to say. How could I have let her go on being poor if I had loved her? When I left for the West I asked that my Provident Fund from the civil service be given to her. But there wasn't much in it. Was that love?

I look at the two of them sitting cross-legged in that harsh, golden light. In this landscape of volcanic rock and round black stones, of sunburnt grass, and the odd eye of green just here and there made possible by effortful irrigation, the three of us could wander anywhere. We would know each inch of soil. Goldie and I used to go for drives and for picnics here. We would eat green *harbara*. In the winter they would roast the tender *bajri* for us. Goldie always liked delicious things to eat, especially tender, green things. Once we went to Goja's village and she cooked a flat, thin omelette for us. We ate it and I felt happy.

Sometimes the uncles—lordlings and princes—would go on deer hunts. That was good too, except the deer got killed. Once I saw Gulba, one of the gunbearers, bash in the head of a wounded deer with a large stone. Blood came out of her mouth.

That's the problem. I can't regress to the past. I can't be a child again. I can't paint it green and golden. Then and now there's always the deer being bashed. I look at Goldie, and realise that for a very long time she too has had a sad and resigned look in her eyes. Not always though. Sometimes she laughs a great roar of a laugh. And Goja strangely doesn't look sad. Like a parrot she looks sometimes, peering at the world, and her lips smile a dolphin smile.

Suddenly Goja says—out of the blue—like the Cheshire cat, "The reason the voices of the poor go unheard is that what the poor have to say isn't acceptable."

17
BORN INTO IT

I've lowered my expectations. It will be enough if Goja, Goldie and I can just be happy in each other's company. I've brought them to the mouth of the little Axe River, close to where I live. Whenever I pass by it I think of Goja and Goldie. It seems to me that they might be sitting there somewhere along the riverbank just out of sight. I explain to them anxiously that I know it's not like the rivers of Maharashtra, but it is very pleasant. (Our rivers are much wider, but they're almost always dry. One could walk across them, except in the rainy season.) There are curlews and oystercatchers in this estuary, I tell them, and sometimes swans glide by. I know it's only tiny, but here even the tiniest streams are called rivers and given names. I like it that even the smallest streams are given names, and in a different mood that would please Goldie as well; but it's clear she has been brooding. Goja and I brace ourselves.

"Does no one need to ask for my forgiveness?" she begins. "Do the rich not suffer? Are the rich godlike?"

"Do they not bleed?" I can hear the echoes. I remember long ago confessing to Goldie I wanted to be a poet. She was amused: so that was what this grandchild wanted. She told me that in that case I would have to search out the heights and depths of the human heart. I wasn't sure I wanted to search the heights and depths—too much blood and palpitating flesh. I wanted to play. But I didn't say so. I decided to try, though perhaps not quite so soon, not just yet. Now, after all these years, I'm willing to hear what's in Goldie's heart, though just at the moment I would have preferred it if she had taken pleasure in the river. At the moment it's reflecting a blue sky and I want to tell them that in England the sky isn't always a dull grey, that the clouds are shape-shifters and the light plays on them; but this isn't the right time.

"Do you seriously expect me to feel sorry for you?" Goja asks Goldie.

This makes me want to defend Goldie. I want to point out that the rich did not stay rich, that in her last days Goldie lived in relative poverty. But it was relative and perhaps Goja would scoff? Still, I don't like to see Goldie scoffed at. I want to point out that in another culture, another time, the fall of a woman of high estate was called tragedy. Well, "man", not "woman", but I'm concerned with Goldie here. I remember the unkempt garden, the reduced entourage. Lear would have wept. But perhaps Goja wouldn't have cared for Lear? And yet there are bits of Goja that are very like Kent. I hold back, hoping that Goldie can take care of herself.

She can. She shrugs and says, "It's not pity I'm looking for, but understanding. I want you to understand with your intellect what it was like to have to be me: the great and golden Ranisaheb, the perfect partner of the kind and kingly Rajasaheb. While the double standard was blazoned unashamedly, I had to maintain a dignified silence and swallow my pride. I was everybody's mother, everybody's grandmother,"—this with a fierce glance at me—"everybody's queen, everybody's matriarch, everybody's—oh, a reincarnation of everybody's goddess of prosperity and wealth. To have outstretched palms thrust at me day in and day out until I was exhausted and had nothing left."

"Hey, hold on," Goja protests. "You had the power to give people things, what do you expect? Look, I'm sorry if you were unhappy, but I can't and don't take any responsibility for your suffering."

"But you expect me to take responsibility for yours?"

"I expect nothing from you," Goja retorts. They're both angry now. I feel I ought to intervene .

"All Goja is saying," I say soothingly, "is that she was born into the set-up. It isn't her fault. There's nothing much she could do about it."

"So was I born into the set-up. There was nothing much I could do about it!" Goldie retorts.

Privately, I think, me too, I was born into the set-up. I got out of it; but I paid a price. I can't decide whether to get involved in the argument or look at the river. The light has changed and is making patterns out of silver and grey. If I look hard, I can just see a heron who is disguised as a piece of wood.

Suddenly Goja says savagely and crudely, "Look, you can't argue that the rich suffer because they're rich. The remedy is easy!"

"The remedy is not easy!" I burst out furiously. "There is a price!"

They stare at me. After everything I've told them, they're still puzzled. They still haven't understood that refusing to be who I was supposed to be wasn't easy. I rage at them, "After everything I've told you, you still haven't understood that refusing to be who I was supposed to be wasn't easy."

They look baffled. "Why didn't you want to be who you

were supposed to be? You could have been happy, comfortable. You would have been here, with us, with me, in the bosom of the family." Goldie is frowning. She looks sad and anxious. "Why did you leave?"

"Oh for pity's sake, Goldie, I was a lesbian and a poet! What did you want me to do? Spend the rest of my life telling lies? I had your talent, your tradition, your genes, but you had educated me in English—I needed *their* language."

"You wanted to escape from us!" Goldie says bitterly.

"Didn't you ever want to escape from us?" I challenge her. "From the squabbling, snivelling children and grandchildren with their countless follies and incessant demands? Didn't you ever want to say, 'Oh for God's sake, grow up and get on with it and have your lives; and leave me free to have my life, to exercise my talents and my genius.' Didn't you ever want to escape from a marriage in which he enjoyed the privileges of men, but you were nailed down to such an extent that you could never forget who you were? Didn't you ever want to escape from that look in people's eyes that made it clear you were somehow above and beyond suffering, that your legs didn't ache, that you didn't weep, and that you did not and could not taste bitter failure; but that if you did, it was what you deserved?"

Goldie looks at me wonderingly. Perhaps I've gone too far. After all, how do I know what it was like for her? And anyway she may not want to disclose her suffering in all its nakedness—it might shame her.

"Do you really think I had talent?" Goldie falters. I'm amazed. Goldie faltering? Being uncertain? I've only seen her approach anything like humility once before—that was when she felt that her death was only a year or two away and she said, "What will become of me? I have not been a good person."

"In your hands," I tell her gently, "language became malleable. You could recite the great Maratha poets. Tukaram, Namdev, Eknath, Shri Jyaneshwar Mauli. I can only recite their names. When you spoke, people listened. It may have been my grandfather who stood for election, but it was you who made the great speeches."

"I wrote nothing, produced nothing, did nothing—a little social work. That's all."

"You were the matriarch. You ruled the family and held it together."

"You escaped!" She sounds unforgiving.

"But the family," I plead with her, "would have swallowed me up. 'We will protect you from anyone and anything outside the family, but within the family we will beat you into shape.' You know that's true. You gave them licence to beat me into shape."

"No one hurt you physically. Besides, it didn't last forever. When you entered the civil service all was forgiven."

"Because then I could be a pillar of the family. Just like you!"

"Yes, like me."

"Goldie, the family wasn't worth it. It ate up your life. As it did Goja's here."

"You were part of that family! It nurtured and protected you."

Both look righteous, indignant and angry, but my own anger rises and bears down on them.

"It didn't protect me! Where were you when that servant molested me?"

"We didn't know" they both protest, "and you didn't tell us."

"Would you have protected me?" I ask bitterly. "Or thrown me to the dogs as a damaged piece of goods!"

"We would have protected you."

I don't believe them.

We sit in silence refusing to cry. The river is smooth and black now. There are only a few slivers of light. The tide has filled it right up to the brim, but it gives no comfort.

"You loved me," says Goldie, "but you went away and wouldn't understand that I was human."

"You loved me," I say, "but you didn't protect me even when I was little."

"You loved me," says Goja, "and let me use up my life being your servant."

It's like a chant. As soon as one of us lets up, another begins.

"I was the Matriarch. That I became old and relatively poor was not convenient."

"I was the Little One. That I ran away was not acceptable."

"I was the Servant. That I had needs of my own was not noticeable."

"If you were really sorry," Goldie says, "you would return."

"If you were really sorry," I say, "you would let me return."

"If you were really sorry," Goja says, "you would do something about the lot of the poor."

You abandoned me.

You neglected me.

You exploited me.

"Stop!" I say to them. "We have to stop this. We have to try to forgive each other." And so, we do try. And some of it is easy enough.

Goja and Goldie say to me, "We loved you, Little One. Forgive us that we neglected you."

And I reply, "I loved you too. I wanted to have my life. Forgive me that I abandoned you."

That part is easy. But when I touch Goja's feet and say to her, "We loved you, Goja. Forgive us that we exploited you," it's not easy at all, and it doesn't work. What opens underfoot is horror.

To say to Goja, "Forgive me that I exploited you, day in and day out, year after year"—that's a travesty. It doesn't make sense. It's not easy.

What do I really want from Goja? And what may I want? I remember the last time I saw her. I touched her feet, but it was to say "Farewell", not to ask for forgiveness. I didn't know it was the last time.

I don't think Goja and Goldie want anything from me. But if it's a question of forgiveness, what's there to forgive? It's not so much a matter of not being angry as of not being frightened. Once the fear goes away, it's not so bad. It's even easy.

The very last time I saw Goldie we both knew it was the last time. I asked her blessing. We didn't cry. I assumed that as a good Maratha that was what Goldie required of me.

18
ROW AWAY BACKWARDS

Why should darkness fall and you recede?
I wanted to send messages like swans
down the river so that as they approached
you'd stretch out your hands in surprised pleasure.
Can't the three of us sit beside a river
and float paper boats inscribed with verse?

But Goldie said:

You must row away even though your face will still be turned towards us. Wave if you like. Islands recede, as do rowing boats. Whatever your fantasies, it's not true that Goja and I necessarily inhabit the same island; though now you've suggested it, we might. When I was alive, I sent you letters, scrawled in handwriting I hoped you could read, written in Marathi I hoped you would understand. They weren't difficult to write, though in time, of course, everything becomes harder. A servant had to fetch pen and paper. You'll say that was easy. It was, but not as easy as it used to be once. Later I had cataracts and had to find someone to dictate to.

Still, writing to you was no hardship. I liked doing it, though the letters were crude. (Yours were no better.) I think mine were like thick slabs of bread, dripping with butter, loaded with honey. No, the queen in her parlour was your fantasy. Oh well, why not? Love doesn't have to be served in tiny quantities like a concentrated chutney on a silver dish. It's such a good product and such a necessary one that children can eat any amount of it and it does them good. Yes, I know, you're thinking of the large slabs of chocolate I used to buy for you when we travelled up to Bombay on the *Deccan Queen*. And yes, I know, chocolate isn't necessarily good for children, but would you rather have had a chocolate-free childhood?

You're no longer a child. I'm no longer alive. Time has passed. That is what you find so hard to accept. You want me to be wise and loving and good, to say something useful. And at the same time you want to be wise, loving and good. Dear one, dear little one, there are some obvious things you are missing. You don't need my wisdom to tell you that, just my friendship. You are not a child, you are grown up. Accept that. I am no longer alive, and being dead is not the same thing as being alive. Accept that. You are ageing. Accept that as well. You must row away backwards.

Am I saying farewell? Because you're alive you must fare forward, you must fare well. We are changeless.

And yet, you changed us. Created Goja, created Goldie. I am not who you thought I was. Do you know which dream I dreamt? Do you know whom I truly loved? No, it was not you, not only you, not necessarily you. Do you know how I built myself, became myself, and slowly disintegrated? You know that I lived. And it mattered to you that I did. That is something. That is enough. But it 's not the truth. And it's not my life.

You're still sitting there, fitfully dipping your oars in the water. You want something. Some piece of wisdom. A message to the world. I wish I could give it to you as easily as a slab of chocolate. Goja gave you dried fish and I gave you slabs of chocolate. I suppose that's significant. But don't you understand? I don't know what will mend the world.

It's not all that easy to foil expectation. My role in life was to accept homage and bless lavishly. The sight of me was supposed to be a good thing—*darshan*. My entrance augured peace and prosperity. It was my name I suppose. I had the name of a goddess and I was a queen, and so people got confused. I was never confused myself, but they weren't to know that. And telling them clearly that I wasn't really better than them wouldn't have been sensible, wouldn't have been politic. Those who thought I was better would have been hurt and disappointed. Why demolish a myth, and with it their satisfaction with their station in life? And those who knew very well that I wasn't better than them would simply have sneered.

You look disappointed. It wasn't worldly wisdom you were looking for, just pure wisdom. I don't have it. It's unreasonable to expect that of the dead, of the old, of your grandmother.

Look, perhaps you had the right idea. Let's write verse, float paper boats, enjoy what there is. Let's play the "do you remember" game and celebrate what there was. Do you remember the *mogra* flowers I loved so much? Does that please you? A list of things I loved? Tender corn. Roasted. With lemon juice and salt and a bit of red pepper rubbed into the cobs. Do you remember how the chap selling them had them perched like parrots on the top of his cart? When my teeth gave way, I still ate corn. Do you remember how the servants used to grate it for me? And I liked sandalwood and incense, but best of all I liked *mogra* flowers. Do you remember how I would go to sleep with a little garland of them tucked under my pillow? When you were very little you used to sleep in my bed. Yes, you too, Little One, I loved you. And things green. Emeralds, green peas, the green woods, the jade green water. In our part of the country—where you grew up and I helped you to grow up, and where I grew up as well—the trees are never particularly green, but even so. Do you remember how we used to eat roasted *bajri*? Delicious. Do you remember the festivals? I liked all of them. I think I liked having so many grandchildren and blessing them all. I suppose there were times when I really thought I was a goddess and where I was there would be fruitfulness and plenty. And there was. Well, why not?

Yes, I know, Goja.

But if there's a problem and an evasion, it's yours. My evasions and my problems are my own now.

Would you like me to bless the world? I will do so lavishly. I will bless the world, and every living creature on it, every bird and beast there ever was. That will take a lifetime, many lifetimes. A worthy occupation. Yes, I could do that. And you? Yes, perhaps you could too. Why not? Merely to observe the excellence of each thing helps and is helpful. But you say it cannot be done without Goja. And that's true too. Without Goja nothing is possible.

19

WHAT GOJA SAID

Do not exploit me again and again. It's tiresome.

You want me to say my own say, have a tongue
of my own, a personal fire. I have no fire.
What's left is grey rock, an obdurate landscape.

Sometimes I hear a craven song. Night recedes,
glows like the blue of a cockerel's feathers
and I stand on a hilltop: dawn's scarecrow.

Caught in the crack between what was
and might have been, no tense applies; all coexist
and any will do.
You say you are lonely?
And that some day you'll join me? I am no
siren, you know. On the other side of death
I 'm nothing and no one. Time has given up—
can no longer kill. And if on a hilltop,
or beside a river, Goldie and I sometimes
take form and gossip a little, where's the harm?
We take nothing away, jostle no one.

But you want me to leave you memories.
The smell of firewood. Grain roasting. The taste
of tobacco on the end of a twig.
What shall I leave you, little one?
My straggly hair? Skinny legs.
Shall I leave you my one-eyed grin?

You say you want to know what it felt like to be me? What it was like to be alive? There are sensations of hot and cold, of being dry or wet, of pressure and the release of pressure. There are surfaces and textures, taste and smell. I'm lying on the floor of a hut, there's the smell of cow dung—pleasant, the floor is plastered with clean cow dung. Ah, to the Western mind it's revolting? But then it's you who are concerned with the Western mind. Not me. And an enormous cockerel is hovering over me—red wattles and all. One beady eye. Russet feathers. Why have the chickens strayed into the hut? Am I edible or not? They peck about for grains. Someone or the other shoos them out.

What is it you want to know? Once I went to work for you and your family there was penury and hardship and a great deal of work. Your lot don't give holidays. There are no holidays. There is no time off. One is a servant for twenty-four hours. You know that. You should understand what your lot thinks. You should understand that we are a function. Not human beings, not women, not creatures—well, creatures perhaps. But for all practical purposes a function. Our purpose is to serve. Should have been robots? How do I know about robots? The dead have an amazing vocabulary. And anyway you know how it is in India—anything is possible, everything happens.

I travelled a great deal with the family. Babysitting, always babysitting. Minding children. In the hot sand at Juhu beach the wind drifts in from the sea. I remember sitting there. I didn't bother to get up to pee. Who needs a penis or a tree trunk? I saw you noticing, Little One. Saw you thinking, "Ah, servants do not wear underpants."

I went to the north, to the great city of Allahabad where the Ganga and Yamuna join. I wanted to bathe in the sacred river, but it wasn't possible. There were always the children, and anyway servants are never off duty. There was no time.

I went to the capital itself, I went to Delhi. I saw the statue of King George and the India Gateway. I thought the statue of King George looked very fine. Well, why not? I had been taught to revere kings, hadn't I?

Do you know where home is, Little One? It's a small village. You've been there. Your grandfather's brother used to live there. It's only a few miles from the main town. So then are we related? Of course not. The Great Gulf fixed. Two different species. All that jazz.

What do you want me to say? Do you want me to be angry? I can't manage it. I don't know why. Beaten out of me. Total exhaustion? The pointlessness of it? Perhaps anger is a luxury indulged in now and then by those who are not poor? What is there to be angry about? When inhumanity reaches such proportions perhaps those who perpetrate it are not human? Would I be angry with a tiger that was eating me? Just afraid and in pain. What would be the point of anger? Of angry explanations to the man-eating tiger? No point. The tiger does what it does. We run about like ants and cockroaches, escape as we're able. Or we run about like humans while an ogre stalks the earth. No, no point.

You want me to say I loved you. You must understand that you were not central to my life in the way you claim I was to yours—except insofar as you were a representative of those who had power. You see, I had my own grandchildren.

Most of this is about you, not me. There's a reason for that. You were rich. I was poor. There, it's been said in all its crudeness. What was life like? Hard, difficult. Enmeshed in poverty. I do not recommend it. Not much to be said. But you want to extract something? Very well, in all that morass there was some kinship and some kindness.

I cannot, and may not, say all is forgotten and forgiven. I will not collude.

20
RIVERS

I've driven to the river in order to find out how this rowing away backwards might be done.

It's only four in the afternoon, but it's close to sundown. The tide has sucked at the estuary until there's almost no water left; but there is a little. Two gulls are floating on the ebbing tide just for fun. Every now and then one of them turns around to look backwards. It seems to me that that gull must be very skilful. At the moment the water is a muted gold—like an emperor's robes. Along the banks and in the sky there are greys and blues and browns and silvers. A heron is fishing further down the bank. It too is blue and grey and brown. Nearer me there are a few herring gulls messing about, and a couple of mallards—nothing exotic. Except me perhaps, but by now even I am commonplace. Just before setting, the sun decides on a burst of splendour and makes a wide path of gold and orange appear in the water. A magpie has been sitting on a branch overhead and ignoring me steadily. A heron just flew across the river. It's November, and by chance it's also Goldie's birthday. If I come this way tomorrow, it will all look different. That's one of the reasons I like it so much.

Once when we were children we stayed at Rajghat on the outskirts of Benares (Varanasi/Kasi) that most sacred and dirtiest of cities. This was soon after my father's death. We had been taken out of the schools we were in; and there was a hiatus, while my mother decided what to do with us. We used to play by the riverbank, until the grownups found out. They told us we absolutely must not wade in the mud. It was filled with germs. The burning *ghat* where they cremated bodies was not far away. Sometimes I could see crows floating down-stream, just resting on the water. I was charmed by them until someone told me that they were sitting on the remains of half-burnt corpses.

Is that what it means to go away backwards? Just float downstream? That can't be what Goldie meant. There was a small boat there which was used as a ferry. The ferryman would let me row the boat sometimes. I thought it was like crossing the bosom of the wide ocean. I couldn't see the other bank.

Goja and Goldie weren't with us, but they would have liked it; and in any case it was the sacred river.

Here by the Axe, I'm neither wading in the river, nor walking away. I'm just sitting here watching the sky change and the gulls muck about. I've always liked watching how the light falls on unstill water. Sometimes on the Canadian lakes I used to pretend to go fishing so that I could sit in a boat and look at the colours shifting in the water. There was one lake called Stony Lake, which had a number of deadheads near the shore. These "deadheads" are the remains of drowned trees. They're like characters in a fairy tale I don't know about—stark and beautiful and very dangerous.

I can't think Goldie meant that I was to forget about her and Goja and stop loving them. I think they both just meant I was to be clear-sighted. And memory is permissible. Anyway, the rivers continue to run whether or not I'm looking at them, the oceans heave, the planets spin—of course they do. There is one thing I would very much have liked Goja and Goldie to see. Also my father. It would have delighted them. I mean the earth as seen from outer space or from the moon—the blue planet with its many oceans. The different shades of blue look so fragile and translucent. I've just realised that I've never seen it. I've only seen photographs. "But that's all right," Goldie and Goja would probably say. "If photographs is all there is, then photographs will do." Goldie liked it when I sent her photographs. I don't think they expect me to talk only about things that are under my nose.

When I was a child we used to go and sit by the local river sometimes. It was the little Banganga, a tributary of the Nira. There was a shrine near it. Usually the river was dry. There were puddles here and there, and I could walk about, and try to catch minnows. In the southern half of India the rivers are often dry except in the rainy season. They're not fed by the melting Himalayan snows like the Ganga, the Yamuna, the Brahmaputra and the Indus (Sindhu). Their names are like poems. But in the rainy season even the rivers of Maharashtra—the word literally means the great country or region—become forceful and rough. When I was in the civil service the dam burst near the city of Pune—Punya Nagar, that name literally means the virtuous city—and the Mula-Mutha River flooded the streets. I stayed up for three nights and days in the Collectorate in order to keep the information coming in about the state of the dam and the measures to be taken. When the dam finally burst I watched the water crawling up the street. Eventually it receded, but the city stank for days afterwards.

I've seen so many different rivers. There's the great Yamuna that flows behind the Taj Mahal. Once when I was very little, I was on a crocodile hunt with my father and a party of other people. I think we were on the Yamuna. I fell off the end of the boat. The water wasn't very deep there and I clambered back in. I remember looking around and thinking, "No crocodiles about," and feeling relieved.

Then there was the great Mississippi. I was impressed in spite of myself. I hadn't wanted to be impressed, because I was having such an unpleasant time in America. Years later my experience of the white-water rapids of the Blue River in Oregon was much better. One of our party fell into the water; but the chap in charge just got out of the boat, hauled the boat back to where she had fallen, and held it there against the current until she was rescued. Along that same river an osprey gave Gill and me a flying demonstration.

And I ought not to forget the muddy Yarra in Melbourne, or the Murray River. That day it had overflowed into the adjoining woods. Gill says that some of the rivers of Australia flow backwards into an inland sea, which no longer exists, and peter out. I find this unlikely, but it may be true. Rivers do extraordinary things. In Toronto the little Don has carved out an enormous valley.

Where I live now there seems to be a little river every few miles. There's the Axe of course, but just next to it there's the Coly, and a little further away there's the Otter. And then further west there are the Sid and the Exe, and to the east there's the Lym. And still further away there's a different Axe River. I went into a cave once at Wookey Hole. They said that was the source of the Axe. For a long time I didn't realise it was a different river. Somewhere there must be the source of this Axe River. People make a pilgrimage to the source of the Ganga in the high Himalayas with great difficulty. I would like to do that, but don't know if I ever will. I like it that the little villages here are named with reference to what the rivers are doing. For instance, Axmouth is at the mouth of the Axe, and Colyford is where you can cross the Coly.

I've been rambling a little, but gradually the rivers have brought me nearer and nearer to the village of Rousdon where I live. Here the river has gone underground, but the sea is nearby, and in the garden there's a little well, which isn't used. Through the window I can see a great pied woodpecker eating peanuts. It's the female this time—no red patch on the back of her head. The peanuts are there for the blue tits and finches; but it's hard not to like the woodpeckers or even the blackbirds. Sometimes a pair of pheasants come. They are ridiculously ornamental, especially the male, and so slow. They're like peacocks in the garden because they look so pretty on the green grass, and they're also like our chickens, the proper colourful Indian ones, because they seem so tame. I want to go out and cluck at them and feed them corn. Goja! Goldie! You would so like them. And you would like the blue tits as well, especially when the sun falls on their little heads and lights up their blue crowns.

It was only yesterday that I drove to the river. There were no swans on display. They were all in the meadow grubbing about. You would laugh to see them. (I suspect them of having pale green underbellies from sitting on the grass so much.) Tomorrow I might go down to the river again. I'll report faithfully on what I see there: the gulls at a conference on the far side of the river, the blue grey heron standing still and trying to catch fish, and also the swans—if there are any. I take my leave of you, but only for the time being.

If you would like to know more about Spinifex Press, write for a free catalogue or visit our Home Page.

SPINIFEX PRESS

PO Box 212, North Melbourne, Victoria 3051 Australia

http://www.spinifexpress.com.au